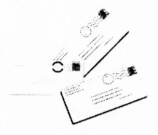

THREE LETTERS FROM TEDDY
and Other Stories

By

Elizabeth Silance Ballard

W0010560

A Righter Book complete and unabridged

Righter Publishing Company, Inc.
PO Box 105
Timberlake, North Carolina 27583

www.righterpublications.com

First Edition
Second Printing
January 2007

Printed *by:*
Lightning Source, Inc.
1246 Heil-Quaker Boulevard
La Vergne, TN 37076

Library of Congress Control Number
2006938430

ISBN: 978-0-9706823-0-7
Three Letters From Teddy and Other Stories
by Elizabeth Silance Ballard

This work was first published by Eslyn
Publishing, Virginia Beach, VA

The Cover

The cover is a photograph taken at the southern end of Laurel Bed Lake, which is located on the top of Clinch Mountain in Russell County in Southwest Virginia. The lake is at 3,732 feet above sea level. The photo was taken mid-October, 2001 when the fall foliage five hundred feet below was at its height of color.

For My Mother

ESTEL STANLEY SILANCE

Who always walked in front of me when I was a child to lead the way and clear the path, and later walked behind me to give me the confidence to forge ahead, and now walks beside me without fail in companionship, friendship, and love.

Table of Contents

Three Letters From Teddy   Page 9

To Wear Big Boots   Page 17

Snowflakes   Page 27

Expectation of a Bright Future   Page 34

The Christmas Nandina   Page 47

Monkey Bread   Page 54

Big Rocks Café   Page 57

A Stranger Named Kenneth   Page 68

Their Special Mother   Page 77

Love Is An Action Verb   Page 84

When Miss Sallie Sang   Page 92

The Mirror   Page 98

Plain Brown Wrapper   Page 106

Something of Value   Page 129

"Teddy had reached a level that would stand him in good stead the following year, no matter where he went"

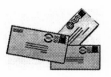

Three Letters From Teddy

Teddy's letter came today and now that I've read it, I will place it in my cedar chest with the other things that are important to my life.

"I wanted you to be the first to know."

I smiled as I read the words he had written and my heart swelled with a pride that I had no right to feel. *Teddy Stallard.* I have not seen Teddy Stallard since he was a student in my fifth-grade class, fifteen years ago.

I'm ashamed to say that from the first day he stepped into my classroom, I disliked Teddy. Teachers try hard not to have favorites in a class, but we try even harder not to show dislike for a child, any child.

Nevertheless, every year there are one or two children that one cannot help but be attached to, for teachers are human, and it is human nature to like bright, pretty, intelligent people, whether they are ten years old or twenty-five. And sometimes, not too often fortunately, there will be one or two students to whom the teacher just can't seem to relate.

I had thought myself quite capable of handling my personal feelings along that line until Teddy walked into my life. There wasn't a child I particularly liked that year, but Teddy was most assuredly one I disliked.

He was a dirty little boy. Not just occasionally, but all the time. His hair hung low over his ears and he actually had to hold it out of his eyes as he wrote his papers in class. (And this was before it was fashionable to do so!) Too, he had a peculiar odor about him that I could never identify.

Yes, his physical faults were many but his intellect left a lot to be desired. By the end of the first week I knew he was hopelessly behind the others. Not only was he behind, he was just plain slow! I began to withdraw from him immediately.

Any teacher will tell you that it's more of a pleasure to teach a bright child. It is definitely more rewarding for one's ego. But any teacher worth his or her credentials can channel work to the bright child, keeping that child challenged and learning, while the major effort is with the slower ones. Any teacher *can* do this. Most teachers *do*, but I didn't. Not that year.

In fact, I concentrated on my best students and let the others follow along as best they could. Ashamed as I am to admit it, I took perverse pleasure in using my red pen; and each time I came to Teddy's papers, the cross-marks (and they were many) were always a little larger and a little redder than necessary.

"Poor work!" I would write with a flourish.

While I did not actually ridicule the boy, my attitude was obviously quite apparent to the class, for he quickly became the class "goat," the outcast--the unlovable and the unloved.

He knew I didn't like him, but he didn't know why. Nor did I know--then or now--why I felt such an intense dislike for him. All I know is that he was a little boy no one cared about, and I made no effort on his behalf.

The days rolled by and we made it through the Fall Festival, the Thanksgiving Holidays, and I continued marking happily with my red pen. As our Christmas break approached, I knew that Teddy would never catch up in time to be promoted to the sixth-grade level. He would be a repeater.

To justify myself, I went to his cumulative folder from time to time. He had very low grades for the first four years, but no grade failure. How he had made it, I didn't know. I closed my mind to the personal remarks:

First Grade: "Teddy shows promise by work and attitude, but he has a poor

11

home situation."

Second Grade: Teddy could do better. Mother terminally ill. He receives little help at home."

Third Grade: "Teddy is a pleasant boy. Helpful, but too serious. Slow learner. Mother passed away end of the year."

Fourth Grade: "Very slow but well behaved. Father shows no interest."

Well, they passed him four times, but he will certainly repeat fifth grade! Do him good! I said to myself.

And then the last day before the holidays arrived. Our little tree on the reading table sported paper and popcorn chains. Many gifts were heaped underneath, waiting for the big moment.

Teachers always get several gifts at Christmas, but mine that year seemed bigger and more elaborate than ever. There was not a student who had not brought me one. Each unwrapping brought squeals of delight and the proud giver would receive effusive thank-yous.

His gift wasn't the last one I picked up. In fact it was in the middle of the pile. Its wrapping was a brown paper bag and he had colored Christmas trees and red bells all over it. It was stuck together with masking tape. "For Miss Thompson--From Teddy."

The group was completely silent and

I felt conspicuous, embarrassed because they all stood watching me unwrap that gift. As I removed the last bit of masking tape, two items fell to my desk. A gaudy rhinestone bracelet with several stones missing and a small bottle of dime-store cologne--half empty. I could hear the snickers and whispers and I wasn't sure I could look at Teddy.

"Isn't this lovely?" I asked, placing the bracelet on my wrist. "Teddy, would you help me fasten it?"

He smiled shyly as he fixed the clasp and I held up my wrist for all of them to admire. There were a few hesitant *ooh's* and *ahh's*, but, as I dabbed the cologne behind my ears, all the little girls lined up for a dab behind their ears.

I continued to open the gifts until I reached the bottom of the pile. We ate our refreshments until the bell rang. The children filed out with shouts of "See you next year!" and, "Merry Christmas!" but Teddy waited at his desk.

When they had all left, he walked towards me clutching his gift and books to his chest.

"You smell just like Mom," he said softly. "Her bracelet looks real pretty on you, too. I'm glad you liked it."

He left quickly and I locked the door,

sat down at my desk and wept, resolving to make up to Teddy what I had deliberately deprived him of -- a teacher who cared.

I stayed every afternoon with Teddy from the day class resumed on January 2 until the last day of school. Sometimes we worked together. Sometimes he worked alone while I drew up lesson plans or graded papers. Slowly but surely he caught up with the rest of the class. Gradually there was a definite upward curve in his grades.

He did not have to repeat the fifth grade. In fact, his final averages were among the highest in the class, and although I knew he would be moving out of the state when school was out, I was not worried for him. Teddy had reached a level that would stand him in good stead the following year, no matter where he went. He had enjoyed a measure of success and as we were taught in our education courses: "Success builds success."

I did not hear from Teddy until several years later when his first letter appeared in my mailbox.

"Dear Miss Thompson,

I just wanted you to be the first to know. I will be graduating second in my class on May 25 from E_____High

14

School.

Very truly yours,
Teddy Stallard"

I sent him a card of congratulations and a small package, a pen and pencil set. I wondered what he would do after graduation. I found out four years later when Teddy's second letter came.

Dear Miss Thompson,

I was just informed today that I'll be graduating first in my class. The university has been a little tough but I'll miss it.

Very truly yours,
Teddy Stallard"

I sent him a good pair of sterling silver monogrammed cuff links and a card, so proud of him I could burst!

And now--today--Teddy's third letter:

"Dear Miss Thompson,

I wanted you to be the first to know. As of today I am Theodore J. Stallard, MD. How about that???!!!

I'm going to be married on July 27 and I'm hoping you to come and sit where Mom would sit if she were here. I'll have no family there as Dad died last year.

Very truly yours,
Ted Stallard

I'm not sure what kind of gift one

sends to a doctor on completion of medical school. Maybe I'll just wait and take a wedding gift, but the note can't wait.

"Dear Ted,

Congratulations! You made it and you did it yourself! In spite of those like me and not because of us, this day has come for you.

God bless you. I'll be at that wedding with bells on!!!"

To Wear Big Boots

His name was Claude which in itself set him apart in the sea of Kevins, Bills, Jims and other more familiar names among the fifth graders who filled my classroom that year. He was a chubby little boy whose head was "buzzed," a hair cut that showed more scalp than hair.

In some years this might not have seemed odd, but that year the little boys were wearing their hair long in the back so poor Claude looked rather alien as he sat at his desk with his head down and shoulders hunched, as if trying to make himself as inconspicuous as possible.

Hunched and quiet as he was, Claude was not inconspicuous because at least once a week he would have a bout with vomiting which sent the little girls into shrieks and one of the boys to fetch the custodian.

At first I attributed the problem to anxiety. Claude was new in our school and was a child who did not make friends easily. I talked to him in what I thought was a loving, caring tone and tried to make him feel comfortable. A few times I even reached down to give him a hug or a pat, but he pulled away each time.

I tried to involve him in small group activities, to help him make contact with other children on a one to one basis. It did not work. Even in close proximity to the others, Claude gave the appearance of being alone, a lost soul drifting in a sea of smiles, carried along on the tides of schoolwork, lunch breaks, and recesses.

As the year wore on, I realized Claude's stomach problems were caused by more than jitters about a new school and made arrangements to talk with his mother. She came at the appointed time, hesitating at my door as if waiting for permission to enter. I tried to put her at ease but she was trembling when she arrived and soon tears streamed as she twisted her pink tissues onto her faded navy skirt.

"I'll try to make things better for Claude," she kept saying.

"Has your family doctor examined your son?" I asked. "I'm really concerned about his frequency of upset stomach episodes."

The young woman before me became even more agitated and a vague uneasiness began to form somewhere deep inside me. Something was terribly wrong. I took her hand in mine.

"Are you all right at home, dear? Is Claude all right?" I asked, silently willing her eyes to meet mine but her hand remained limp as she continued to stare at her skirt.

18

"Everything's fine," she said. "Is it okay if Claude brings some Pepto Bismol to school with him? He says the boys and girls are cruel to him when he vomits."

I said he could bring the medication and made a mental note to speak to the school nurse. As I watched the young woman walk away from me, hunched over as I had seen Claude hunched so many times--I knew Pepto Bismol wouldn't solve Claude's problems--or hers.

Little changed after Claude's mother came to school. I did notice that he wore a new sweater the next week and the latest fad on his feet. Claude was excited about the new shoes and seemed almost perky, but the vomiting was still a weekly event and I was still worried.

"Something is definitely wrong," the school nurse agreed, "but I don't know what. He doesn't talk when he comes here to rest after his vomiting episodes. He won't lie down either. He just sits for a few minutes and then asks to return to class."

Something more needed to be done so I sent a note home with Claude asking parental consent for Claude to talk with the school counselor. I got my answer the next afternoon.

"Who do you think you are, lady?" he yelled, stomping into my room in his big

19

black boots.

I didn't need to ask his name. The shirt of his uniform bore a nametag. It was Claude's stepfather.

He told me loudly and in no uncertain terms that I should mind my own business, that Claude did not need a counselor but was "just a weak, sniveling crybaby! So back off! Do your job! Teach!"

With that he stormed past several teachers gathered outside my door and the next morning, Friday, Claude did not come to school. I was frantic until Monday when my anxiety reached a new level. Bruises were evident on the boy's neck and he vomited three times before lunch. I asked my aide to take charge while I took Claude to the nurse.

He paled when she asked him to raise his shirt and refused until we called in the principal, Mr. Meadows. Claude gave in then and showed us the welts on his back. He spoke not a word and his face was devoid of emotion. His body was there but somehow Claude had left us. That afternoon a report was filed with Child Protective Services.

The next day Claude's seat was empty again and it stayed empty the rest of the year. The family simply disappeared and when I cleaned out his desk, I found all his books. Claude had known he would not be returning to my class.

His school records were requested the next fall from somewhere in Texas and it was nine years before I heard of Claude again. I was watching the evening news and suddenly there he was, older, but still recognizable.

"A Texas man killed his stepfather today...." the announcer was saying.

Man? Claude was barely 18 and I listened in horror over the next few days as the story unfolded telling of the sexual abuse I had not recognized or even suspected. I tried to remember every single detail about Claude, but the only thing that seemed to relate was Claude's refusal to lie down on the health room cot and the fact that he never wanted anyone to touch him. Was that enough to alert either the nurse or me to the situation? The guilt for my lack of recognition weighed heavily and I had trouble sleeping, eating and meeting my classes.

The case did not make the television news after those first few days following the arrest and I could find nothing in the papers about it but I couldn't let it go. I needed answers.

What telltale signs had I missed?

What? I asked myself over and over.

Finally I arranged for a substitute teacher, booked my flight and a few days later I was in a Texas jail. As I stood there, awaiting permission to see him, the thought occurred to me that he might not remember me. Even worse, he might remember me but refuse to see me.

"Right this way, Ma'am."

I followed the deputy into the room where he said I might speak with Claude.

"I'll have to stand here in the room with you, Miss Thompson," he said.

They brought Claude in to sit opposite me at the stained and scratched table.

He was perplexed at my being there.

"Did you move out here from North Carolina, Miss Thompson?"

I explained that I had come especially to see him, that I was hurt and bewildered by all that had happened and that I needed to know how I had failed him.

"According to the news, Claude, you were suffering horrible abuse during the time you were in my classroom. What did I miss? What should have alerted me? Help me not to fail the next child in my class who might be suffering as you did."

He looked down at his hands clasped there on the table, and in spite of myself, I began to cry. In that tall young man lurked the little boy who still hunched over, trying to make himself small and inconspicuous. My tears disturbed him.

"Miss Thompson, there's no way you could have known. You tried to help me. I knew back then that you were trying to help me, but...."

We held hands tightly. I could not speak.

"The vomiting," he whispered. "I'm sorry about that, Miss Thompson, but I couldn't help it. He--well, you probably know all about it from the news. I'm sure everybody knows by now, but he--well, he would hold my head and make me--well, you know what he made me do. It was in the news. I don't want to talk about that, Miss Thompson, but I just wanted you to understand about the vomiting.

"I would be sitting in class, you know, and you would be going over spelling words or something and I would think about what had happened the night before, what he had made me do, and I would just vomit. The kids were cruel, Miss Thompson, but you were always nice. Don't think you weren't. You were always nice to me."

Cold and trembling with shame and rage, I tried to stay calm. Nice? I was nice to him? I was nice but this child went through several more years of brutish treatment no child should experience because I hadn't even suspected.

"What price ignorance," I said aloud.

"It's okay, Miss Thompson," he said, squeezing my hand. "Don't blame yourself."

"It's not okay, Claude! I was ignorant. Ignorant and naive! I'm so sorry, Claude. I'm so terribly sorry."

They led him away after an awkward hug between us and I felt rooted to the spot. And old. I felt very old.

"Come on, Miss Thompson." The deputy was holding my arm.

I nodded and thanked him as he helped me into the cab, which would take me to the airport. So now, here I sit, the drone of the plane's engines doing nothing to drown out the self-accusations I hear screaming in my head.

I must go back to class tomorrow. I must go back to class and I must start looking at each child differently. I must *really* look. And I must listen. And I must not be afraid to ask questions, to probe, to accuse, if necessary! I must be a watchdog. I must learn to see the ugliness around me and I must learn to yell--yell until someone listens. I, too, must learn to wear big boots.

"Instead of exploring Alicia's world, I expected her to conform to mine as outlined in my lesson plans and schedule book."

Snowflakes

The room was chaotic that day. Everywhere I looked there were paints, doilies, and colorful paper chains. Around and through it all my boys and girls scooted from one project to another, excited in their effort to transform our ordinary classroom into the prizewinner of a Christmas decorating contest. There was only one exception.

"Alicia Fairway!"

She looked up, dropping her book to the floor. Then she fell out of her chair reaching for the book and everyone laughed. Everyone except Alicia and me.

"Alicia, why aren't you with the others?" I snapped. "You're letting your group down. Look how hard Diane and Sue Ellen are working to paint a lovely window while you just sit here!"

"I was reading," she mumbled, but she sauntered over to the window and took up a brush with white paint to dab a few snowflakes on the Christmas scene in progress.

"Miss Thompson! Alicia is painting snowflakes! There weren't any snowflakes in Bethlehem! Were there, Miss Thompson?"

I glanced at Alicia.

27

"There should have been," she said. "Snowflakes are pretty."

"Alicia, paint what your group voted to paint."

She picked up her brush again but her heart wasn't in it and I felt a momentary stab of guilt for scolding her. Why did she resist any effort on my part to engage her in class activity? Why was her nose always in a book?

Now, ordinarily I rejoice when I see a child taking an interest in reading, but this child--well, that's ALL she wanted to do. If I would try to go over spelling words, she was reading a book she had sneaked from the classroom library shelf.

"I already know all the words, Miss Thompson," she would mumble and I didn't doubt it. Alicia had never made less than a perfect score on a spelling test.

If the class was reviewing a math test, Alicia would be engrossed in a book she had brought from home.

"But I made a hundred on that test, Miss Thompson."

This went on again and again that year and I began to realize that Alicia was retreating from all of us into her world of books and nothing I tried seemed to make a difference. My patience was wearing thin. I hoped that after Christmas I would be ready

28

to tackle the next semester with some new ideas, that I would be able to bring her out of her shell.

I thought about Alicia a lot over the holidays. Being single, I usually spent Christmas Day with my sister and her children, but my students were MY children and most of my life was spent preparing to teach, teaching, studying, or working out solutions for my problem students. Alicia definitely took up a lot of my thinking time that Christmas.

After the holidays everything was business as usual in our classroom with Alicia in her own world while the rest of the class moved on according to my schedule. I had obviously not rested enough over the school vacation because I found myself snapping more and more at Alicia and the other children quickly picked up on it, setting themselves up as--well, tattletales.

"Miss Thompson, Alicia is reading again!" They would yell and my nerves seemed to stretch a little tighter each day.

What kind of teacher AM I? I wondered.

Obviously, not a good one! I answered myself. I was giving my class the idea that reading was not a good thing; I had made a child into the butt of tattling and taunting by others; I was punishing her for doing something I normally reward students for; and, all the while I knew something serious was bothering Alicia, was driving her deeper within herself and away from the outside world.

Since her escape appeared to be within the pages of her books, I decided to keep track of what she was reading.

We were at recess that afternoon and all the others were playing dodge ball. Alicia sat on the cafeteria steps reading. I sat down beside her.

"What are you reading?" I asked.

She wordlessly showed me the book but I felt as if I had just been reprimanded for interrupting.

"Don't you want to play dodge ball, Alicia?"

She shook her head. There was nothing more to be said unless I was going to say it. I was angry, though I did not for the life of me know why.

"What types of books do you like best?" I asked.

She slowly reached into the pocket of her jeans and brought forward a folded, dog-eared piece of notebook paper on which was listed every book, by date and author, that she had read that year. I was astounded at the number as well as her record keeping. And the variety of books was surprising: Biographies, fiction, poetry, non-fiction in the areas of science and history--some books well beyond her grade level.

"Maybe I should have assigned more book reports this year!" I said, smiling at her as I stood to leave.

When we got back into the room, Alicia brought a large spiral-bound notebook to my desk.

"What's this?" I asked briskly, eager to get to the next stage of my lesson plan for the day.

"Book reports," she said. "I write book reports on all the books I read. Do you want them?"

I noticed that she held another notebook. "Is that another set of book reports?"

"No, Ma'am," she said. "These are my stories. The ones I wrote. Do you want them, too?"

She shyly held it out to me, obviously with some reservation. It was the first time this child had reached out to me in any way and I did not want to blow this opportunity to make real contact.

"Yes, I do," I whispered. "Let's read them together during free time." That afternoon, Alicia read her collection of

31

essays and short stories to me and I knew why I had not been able to reach this little girl. I had reached out on the wrong level. All those months I had tried to make her fit the mold, to blend in, to be like the others when all the time she was on another level, in a realm of her own imagination. She read not to escape or to retreat from the world around her. She read because it caused her own imagination to take flight.

I had fallen into the trap of thinking that *different* meant *wrong*. Instead of exploring Alicia's world, I had expected her to conform to mine as outlined in my lesson plans and schedule book.

I gave her average teaching while she struggled against great odds to be herself which meant not average. In my zeal to find psychological problems, I had almost created problems where none existed.

For the rest of that year, I had dual lesson plans and a dual schedule. Alicia didn't need to conform. Alicia needed to soar and she needed a teacher who could soar with her.

Alicia's parents compiled her original works and found a local printer who produced several copies of *Snowflakes*. They surprised me with a copy at the end of the year and it's still in my bookcase right beside her next book, which was just published last year by a well-known publisher.

I saw her recently and she is still the same quiet, introspective person I knew many years ago, going her own way oblivious to what is "expected" and what others are doing. Alicia is still soaring.

Expectation Of a Bright Future

"Look for something good in every bad situation, Mona, and you will never be defeated," Mama always told me. When Charlie died, there was no good to be found and I was sure nothing good would ever happen for me again.

I was making cherry cobbler that afternoon and the scent of the simmering red cherries was strong when Mama came through my back door, her eyes brimming with tears. My heart began to pound.

"Mona, it's Charlie," she said. "They tried to reach you from the shop but your phone has been busy."

Stunned, I saw that Jill had not quite replaced the phone in its cradle when she called her friend that morning before school.

"Charlie's been hurt? Did they take him to the hospital?" I began looking for my handbag and keys. "I've got to get over there!"

Mama took my arm and led me to the den.

"Let's sit down, Mona."

Then she told me: Charlie was dead.

Charlie dead? Gone? Just like that? My husband had left home that morning for his job as a front-end mechanic, whistling like always, and now he was gone? I tried

34

to concentrate, to remember what I had said to Charlie as he left that morning, to remember if I had kissed him good-bye but Mama wouldn't stop talking.

"....an accident at the shop. They say he couldn't possibly have felt anything. It all just happened so fast."

I watched Mama remove the pot of cherries from the stove and turn the knob to "off."

"There must be some mistake....."

"There's no mistake," Mama whispered. "I'm so sorry. I loved Charlie, too."

Yes, Mama loved my husband now though she certainly had her doubts years before when I had announced that Charlie and I were getting married.

"It's too soon, Mona," she had told me. "Neither of you are out of your teens yet. It doesn't matter so much with you because you're very mature, but boys--and Charlie is still a boy, mind you! --Well, when they get tied down too soon, they are likely to....."

She had been wrong, though. Charlie was a wonderful husband, a real family man. A loving and playful father for Betty Sue and Jill. And now.....

"No matter how bad things are, no matter how much you hurt, Mona, something good will come from this. You just mark my words. Something good will come of all this."

I couldn't answer. I couldn't say anything or even feel anything. It was as if somehow I were wrapped in a cocoon, an invisible cocoon, a safe place where no feelings could reach me.

The next few days were filled with family and friends bringing food and what they probably thought was comfort. Then the funeral and that night my cocoon disintegrated and the enormity of Charlie's death rushed in on me. I smiled as I tucked the girls in but as I lay alone, I knew Mama was wrong--nothing good could come from the intense loneliness and grief or from the fear now taking control.

I had never worked in my life. Charlie and I had married three days after our high school graduation and I became pregnant almost immediately. Even though I was happy as a full-time mother all those years, I now had no skills, no training, no education. How was I to support my little girls and myself?

"What about life insurance?" Mama asked, as we sat a few days later looking through business papers, our checkbook and Charlie's will.

I hated to tell her there was no

insurance. Charlie had just changed jobs and wasn't yet eligible for benefits with the new company.

"We let the old policy lapse. We thought we couldn't afford it," I admitted. "After all, Charlie was young and healthy and........"

What could I say? Another bad decision we had made.

"The house payment is due next week," Mama said. "Here's the coupon book."

There was no way I could make payments on the doublewide mobile home we had purchased just the previous summer but Mama had a suggestion.

"Why not trade for a smaller model with smaller payments?"

We talked to the dealer the very next day but without a job I couldn't qualify for the loan. My only alternative was to move in with Mama until I could find work and get on my feet. I put a *For Sale* sign in the yard and began packing.

"Move to Granny's? That old place?" Betty Sue wailed. "Mom, it doesn't even have an air conditioner!"

I tried to present the facts without causing them excessive worry as the home we had enjoyed moved out of our lives as quickly as Charlie had. One day we still lived there and the next day the neighbors helped me move everything to the farmhouse where I had spent my childhood. For months I rarely left it.

It was all I could do to drag myself out of bed every morning. As soon as my eyes opened, the tears would begin to flow and I felt I just couldn't get through another day without Charlie. Even getting myself dressed was a chore so Mama would get the girls off to school. I had no energy for anything.

"You need to get your mind on something else, Mona. You need to keep busy."

So Mama bought new patterns and fabric so I could begin sewing again. I normally loved to sew for the girls but I just couldn't seem to concentrate.

"Depression. It's to be expected but maybe this will help," Dr. Street said, handing me a prescription.

It didn't help. After paying the receptionist for my office visit, there was no money left for the pharmacy. I never even told Mama I had gone to the doctor. We weren't getting along too well by that time.

It had been a long time since she had to live with children and though Mama was good to Betty Sue and Jill, it was obvious they got on her nerves. She never said anything to them but she became increasingly impatient with me and we began bickering and the more we bickered, the angrier I got. Angry at her, at myself, and even at Charlie.

Why did you have to be the one to crawl under that car? It was your lunch hour! Why didn't you just leave? I screamed at Charlie silently in the darkness of my bedroom.

"Where is the insurance?" I would ask Charlie in my dreams, hitting him again and again, then waking up filled with guilt. I loved Charlie and missed him so much. Why was I so angry with him?

I was angry at myself, too. Angry at my lack of education and work experience that would have helped support my children. I was angry morning, noon and night but I didn't cry anymore and I was tired of Mama telling me I ought to get out and be with people.

"Maybe you're right!" I yelled at her one day. "Anything would be better than staying in this place listening to you criticize me all the time!"

I began going out but I felt terrible about it. Charlie was gone but I still felt married so I was burdened with guilt every time I walked out the door. I made myself do it though and Mama quit fussing--for a while.

"I wish you would put as much energy into finding a job as you do into socializing," she told me one day as I dressed for a movie with friends. "It's time to get hold of yourself, Mona. You're a mother. Act like one! Betty Sue and Jill have lost their father. Don't let them lose their mother, too.

"I don't mind your being here, Honey, but you three need to become a family again. I need to have two grandchildren and a grown daughter, not three children."

Her words cut deep. I wanted to tell her to mind her own business, but it WAS her business. I had moved my family into her home.

"Try to understand how I feel, Mama! I've lost my husband. I've lost my home. I can't find a job and, YES, I've looked! I've applied for many jobs. Nobody wants me! I have nothing to offer!"

It was true. I had applied again and again but I just didn't get hired. No experience, no training and no skills.

I continued to fill out job applications, but precious few interviews resulted and no job offers were made.

Mama and I had always been close but our relationship was stretched to the breaking point. She wanted me to take control of my life and my children again and I wanted to do that but I just couldn't seem to get a grip on things. My self-esteem was lower than it had ever been. I felt worthless.

Then one night at a church supper, Miss Violet Thompson sat down next to me. Miss Thompson had been my fifth grade teacher but now she was teaching second grade. Both my girls had been in her class.

"Mona, you're too smart to be wasting your life like you're doing," she said as casually as if she were talking about the weather.

How dare she talk to me like that? I thought to myself. I wasn't a child in her class anymore and I wanted to make some sarcastic retort. The words just wouldn't come though and Miss Thompson just kept on talking.

"You've done so well with your little girls, Mona. They're always clean and neat and have such good manners. When each of them came through my class they always had their homework done and were always prepared for tests."

I looked away. Couldn't she see I wanted to be left alone?

"Not all pupils who come through

41

my class have the type of mothering you give your girls. Some women don't know how. Some don't want to do it and some are too tired after working one, often two, jobs to do it. And, of course, some aren't there to do it."

I hated myself for just sitting there, saying nothing, feeling as if I were back in elementary school, being chastised by the teacher.

".......and so I was wondering, Mona, if you wouldn't like to come help in my classroom as a volunteer for those children who need that kind of attention. Just until you find work, of course. I have three or four children now who need help with their reading, spelling, table manners, social behavior, even their hair."

"Their hair?" I asked, dumbfounded.

"Oh, yes. Children who haven't been taught the basics of hygiene, good grooming and acceptable social behavior start school with a strike against them. They realize something is wrong but they don't know what. They just know they are different somehow, not accepted the way they want and need to be if they are to develop confidence. And confidence they must have if they are to have any expectation of a bright future."

I started visiting Miss Thompson's

42

classroom one or two days a week, then I was there every day. The four children with whom I worked were sullen and suspicious at first and I was awkward and unsure of myself. As I began to love and appreciate them, though, they began to respond.

"They're going to hire three teacher's aides for the fall term, Mona," Miss Thompson said to me one Friday afternoon as we walked to the faculty and staff parking lot. "I think you ought to apply."

"But I don't have the certificate that's required," I reminded her.

"I think they might make an exception in your case if you'll enroll for courses at the community college. Your experience and success in my class will more than make up for the certificate you lack and you can get that by attending classes at night while working here during the day. What do you think?"

Well, ten years have passed now and my first little group of second graders are now graduating. Of those four boys and girls, one moved away and three of them are still in town. All three will be going to college in the fall.

"You helped make that possible, Mona," Miss Thompson told me. "Every one of those children were already potential drop-outs or worse by the time they had reached our second grade class. You gave them pride and self-assurance. They began to see themselves as special people because you thought they were special."

I am proud of them and of my own two daughters, too. Betty Sue is a Licensed Practical Nurse now and Jill is taking, of all things, air-conditioning and refrigeration repair courses at the community college. She has Charlie's mechanical ability.

When she enrolled, I thought of the day I told them we would be moving to their grandmother's home and they were upset because there was no air-conditioner in the house. I guess Jill decided she would never be without air-conditioning again!

Mama died two years ago, but not before she saw me being presented Sheffield County's Teacher's Aide of the Year award. She said it was one of her happiest moments.

"I was so upset when you married Charlie right out of high school," she confessed that night. "And I was really afraid for your future when he died but you have done well and you've made an impact on so many children."

And I owe it all to Miss Violet Thompson.

I've never really been sure if Miss

Thompson needed me in her class that first year or if she saw a young mother floundering in life and cared enough to help. I have a hunch she saw I had lost my own expectation of a bright future and simply stepped in to help me regain it.

Mama meant well when she told me to look for the good even in the bad times following Charlie's death; but, Miss Thompson knew that we sometimes hurt too much to see good in situations and that we sometimes need help to prevent defeat. We need someone to reach out with warmth and caring the way Miss Thompson did for me and as I try to do for the children who enter our second grade classroom every September.

"Mom went to sleep lying on the sofa, watching the tiny lights twinkle on the nandina bush..."

The Christmas Nandina

Nandina: *"Nan-deena"* *An evergreen shrub with red berries used by the Norbert family as a tabletop Christmas tree." Paul Norbert*

Nandina: *"Nan-deena" A very lovely evergreen bush with red berries which should stay in the yard and is definitely NOT a Christmas tree." Anne Norbert.*

Anne and Paul had their first marital spat on December 15, three months after the wedding. Anne had been making exquisite lace ornaments for weeks and now she wanted to buy their first Christmas tree, a special tree, one they would always remember.

"But we already have our Christmas tree," Paul told her, and he went to the patio to get the nandina bush.

"A bush?" she asked, laughing, believing he must be teasing her. "A bush in a black plastic pot?"

But Paul was not teasing.

"The Norberts always have a nandina bush at Christmas. I guess I should have told you sooner but it never occurred to

47

me because it's just something we've done since I was twelve years old. It's our holiday tradition now and I won't change it."

Anne's face flushed. Oh, the nandina bush was pretty in its own way. It had been out on their patio since the day after their wedding when Paul had moved his things from the apartment he shared with his brothers. Pretty as it was, though, it was not a Christmas tree. It was not something she wanted to place her lovely handmade ornaments on and it would hardly hold even one string of the tiny white lights.

"But why, Paul? Why?"

"Listen, Anne," he said. "Dad died when Davey was two years old and Mom did her best for the next three years. Then she got sick."

Anne listened as Paul went on to explain that his mother, Julia, had lost so many hours at the hosiery mill due to her illness that what little she had been able to provide for her three sons deteriorated rapidly. Mounting medical bills took priority as she tried desperately to get well.

"That was the first year we did not have a Christmas tree," he said, holding Anne close. "Randy was eight; Davey was five; and I was twelve--and disgusted. I wanted a Christmas tree. All my friends had

48

one and I was angry that we couldn't have one, too.

"Well, a week before Christmas Mom came home from her doctor's visit and told me she needed surgery and that she would be going into the hospital on December 26. She said she had been hoping to work extra hours but she hadn't been able to do that."

"I'm going to need your help, Paul, to make Christmas special this year," she had told her oldest son.

Resentfully, Paul had listened to his mother's idea and helped her dig up the nandina bush from the yard and put it in a black plastic pot.

"I've always loved nandinas," she had said. "My grandmother had nandinas in her yard back in Virginia and there were always lovely red berries at Christmastime. See how many berries there are? They'll show up pretty if you and the boys put a few lights on it."

Paul thought of the tall trees with glittering ornaments and stars his friends had described and the nandina bush seemed a poor substitute.

"We tried to decorate it to look like a real Christmas tree and Randy and Davey thought it was great fun. Davey was too young to remember the Christmas trees we

49

had in the past and Randy was always good-natured and eager to please so he didn't even question this strange substitute. No, I was the only one who hated the thing."

Julia had made it clear she understood Paul's anger and disappointment but she went on with her arrangements-- packing a small bag for the hospital and trying to prepare food for them to have until she could get back home.

"On Christmas Eve morning we all walked the six blocks to church with us boys fussing when we had to stop several times to let Mom rest. When we finally reached the stone steps she told me to stay outside with my brothers until she came back."

After a while Paul began to get anxious. People were arriving for the special children's service and to see the living nativity on the church lawn.

"My brothers were restless and started arguing. Angry that I had been left outside with them, I went to find Mom."

Paul had wandered through the halls until he heard his mothers voice, talking softly and crying. It was something he had never seen his mother do.

"...and--well, if anything happens to me, my boys..."

Paul's heart pounded as he stood listening.

"My oldest one, Paul--well, he's had to help me so much since I've been sick. I really...."

"It wasn't until then that I knew Mom was much sicker than I had realized and that she was very worried about us. I slipped back outside and told the boys that I couldn't find her and when she came out she was smiling. Randy and Davey didn't even notice that her face was swollen and her eyes still teary and we all went inside for the children's Christmas Eve service as if nothing were wrong."

Paul had no idea when they were delivered, but the next morning there had been several gifts piled on the table by the nandina bush. There was one for each of them from Julia, and the others from their friends at church.

"There were two gifts for me," Paul said, smiling at the memory. "A Scrabble game and a book, a Hardy Boys mystery. I still have them."

Julia had lain on the sofa all smiles as the little boys screeched in the delight of ripping the bright wrapping paper. She had made their favorite breakfast--hot chocolate and monkey bread.

"Later in the morning, Randy's Sunday school teacher brought a huge tray of turkey, dressing, and a bag of other good

51

things we had not seen for a very long time. After Randy and Davey went to bed that night, Mom gave me a pen and paper and asked me to write a thank-you note to our church who had provided for us on such short notice when she had been unable to do so herself.

"Mom went to sleep lying on the sofa, watching the tiny lights twinkle on the nandina bush while I sat at the kitchen table rewriting the thank-you note she had dictated so that it would be neat as she insisted.

"The next day she went to the hospital and she never came home. That was the first Christmas 'tree' that Davey would remember and it was the last one we had with Mom. We came to Virginia to live with Aunt Louisa who loved us and helped us through that first lonely, frightening year. Most of all she understood why, the following Christmas, we insisted on decorating the nandina bush we had brought from home.

"I love you, Anne, but in this one thing I won't give in."

Anne nodded, unable to speak, now seeing beyond the simple little bush to the love of a mother long departed who had left three sons behind, each possessing her quiet strength and tenderness. Julia had bequeathed to them a legacy of love, which now included Anne, and would include the children of Paul and Anne who were yet to come; children with whom they would share each year the story of the Christmas nandina.

Julia's Monkey Bread

4 cans of refrigerator biscuits (10 each)

1 3/4 cups sugar
3/4 cup margarine
2 tsp. cinnamon

Julia always let Paul mix the sugar and cinnamon. Randy and Davey would tear each biscuit into four pieces. (After washing hands very well, of course!) All three boys rolled the pieces in the cinnamon/sugar mixture and dropped them into a greased and floured bundt pan. (A tube pan can also be used.)

Julia would then mix the melted margarine into the remaining cinnamon/sugar mixture and pour evenly over the biscuit pieces.

It baked at 325 degrees for 45-50 minutes and then set for 10 minutes before Julia turned it out of the pan. Yum! Yum! The Norbert boys enjoyed pulling the monkey bread apart rather than using a knife to cut it. That's the fun of monkey bread! But Julia always kept wet washcloths close by for all those sticky fingers!!

"A faithful friend is the medicine of life."
Ecclesiastes 6:16

Big Rocks Cafe

The sign said "Big Rocks Cafe" and those who didn't know any better, those who were first-timers or who had just stopped in to ask directions, thought it was named for the two thirty pound rocks perched precariously on a shelf over the outdated cash register.

"Came from the North Pole. These rocks are always cold," they were told upon inquiry. "Carried them in my sea bag all the way. Feel. They're cold, just like I told you."

Patrons would carefully reach up high to rub the gray cold hardness and ponder the pink streaks circling the rocks. They were eye-catchers all right, but actually the café was named for Rockford K. Lancaster, the owner, a hulk of a man who stood six foot four and who was generally known as Big Rock.

"Just couldn't think of a real name for the place," he would say by way of explanation.

"But why don't you put an apostrophe on your sign?" Someone once asked him, someone not from the neighborhood.

"Everybody knows this is Big Rock's place and that I'm Big Rock."

And that was that. Big Rock was not a man who was concerned with trifles like apostrophes and it was true that everybody-- at least everybody in Big Rock's world, which was that six-block area of the city called Pine Ridge--knew who Big Rock was and where his place was.

Some said Big Rock had been a cook in the Navy back in World War II but no one really knew for sure because Big Rock never talked about himself. He spent his days listening to his customers talk about their lives, laughing at their jokes and patting their backs (literally and figuratively) when they were down on their luck. When the focus turned to Big Rock, when someone asked a question about his life outside the cafe, Big Rock conveniently remembered something that needed doing in the kitchen.

Big Rock was comfortable with the man he had become and the life he had made for himself. His days and his customers were predictable and he liked that. Most of his day customers were people who still worked in the deteriorating neighborhood, whose employers were not prosperous or ambitious enough to move across town. They came in for coffee and cigarettes during their breaks or at lunch time for soup and Big Rock's own special sandwiches, so thick they were difficult and often embarrassing to eat if you were concerned with good table manners (which most people were not at the Big Rocks Cafe, even the normally well-mannered ones.)

After 3:30 P.M., the place would be filled with neighborhood children and teens sipping sodas, laughing and talking, some even doing homework in the back booths. They didn't buy much, but Big Rock didn't mind.

He knew these kids did not have money, that the only kids who had money in that neighborhood were the ones who got it by--well, Big Rock didn't want to even think, much less *say* it aloud. He only knew that these kids in his place were okay and if they felt good being there, if they needed a place to hang out away from the other kind, he would see to it they had it.

By five o'clock the kids were gone and that was Big Rock's favorite time of the day when those who lived in the aging, hot and dreary apartment buildings nearby would drop in for refreshment to help them make the daily transition from jobs which bent their backs to the homes which bent their spirits.

A few laughs at Big Rocks got most of them in a better frame of mind though, made it a little easier to face the drabness of home and the never-ending needs of their

59

families which they just couldn't seem to meet no matter how hard they tried. It was mostly the same crowd, congenial and comfortable, which had become a sort of extended family to each other over the years and, like most families, they had their favorite member--an unkempt, shaggy man known as "Yogi Bear" Hobson, nicknamed for his favorite cartoon character.

Big Rock had become quite fond of Yogi over the years, perhaps it could be said that he even loved Yogi as he would a brother, a brother who had fallen short of his goals in life. In fact, everybody seemed to have a special liking for Yogi though they had since forgotten his real name and none of them knew exactly where he lived or worked. He said he painted houses sometimes and did a little carpentry work here and there.

"Whatever and wherever I can make a dollar or two," Yogi told them and a dollar or two was all Yogi ever seemed to have but it didn't seem to bother him any. He seemed satisfied to wear the same few clothes day after day and was never heard to complain or wish for anything he did not have.

Of course, about all anyone could say about his clothes was that they *covered* him and Yogi's hair looked so bad that Big Rock brought in a pair of scissors one night and told Yogi he was going to cut his hair. From that time on, Big Rock was Yogi's personal barber and no one could deny that Yogi's hair did look--well, *shorter!*

Sometimes Big Rock wondered why they all liked Yogi so much. He never smiled, hardly ever talked and even got downright rude when people got too noisy while he was trying to watch his cartoons. Yet, there was something about Yogi that drew people to him, made them want to do things for him. Maybe it was the lost, distant look in his eyes or the deep lines covering his face, which spoke of a life that had not been kind, even less kind than their own.

Maybe it was the fact that here was somebody with even less than they had, that no matter how hard times got, no matter how empty their wallets were, no matter how little they had or were likely to have, here was someone who had less. Maybe it wasn't so much that they *liked* Yogi as it was that they needed him.

Over the years they bought him beers when he was between jobs, shared their cigarettes and conceded that the seat at the end of the counter nearest the TV was his. When Big Rock saw him coming, he would twist the dial to Yogi's favorite station and would often slip a plate on the counter filled with steaming soup and a roast beef on rye or a hot dog with chili and onions, Yogi's favorites.

"Help me out with this, Yogi. I've overcooked again and you know I can't stand to waste food," he would say.

Sometimes Yogi would protest, being out of work and money, and Big Rock would have to say, "Oh, go ahead, Yogi. You know your credit is good with me."

So, Yogi, to stop the hunger pains in his belly would eat the meal in front of him, eyes steady on the hot, steamy food, shoulders hunched in a way that invited no further conversation.

In time, though, Yogi began to eat less and less and Big Rock became worried.

"You know," he said one night to some of the crowd, "I think Yogi is sick."

It was generally decided that something had to be done, his family located, some medical help found for him, but they weren't sure just how to go about it. "I don't even remember his real name," Big Rock said. "I'm not sure he even remembers it. I asked him one day what his real name was and he just looked at me as if I were crazy. Said his name was Yogi--just Yogi."

All efforts to obtain information about Yogi's family were futile.

"No family," he said. "Just me-- Yogi."

Finally they gave up trying and assumed the responsibility for Yogi's medical help. A collection was taken up to help Big Rock who had personally taken Yogi to the doctor, then to the hospital where it was determined that Yogi had cancer.

"It's why he won't eat," Big Rock explained, not really understanding it himself.

He took plates to the hospital filled with all the things he knew Yogi liked best, but Yogi just ate less and less and grew thinner and weaker.

They all rallied to Yogi, taking turns trying to make him laugh, eat and talk; but, in the end it was Big Rock who was sitting by his bed and holding his hand when Yogi simply closed his eyes and left Big Rock sitting alone, trembling as the tears rolled down into the heavy scruff of beard.

"He died easy," he told the crowd back at the cafe and they began collecting for Yogi's funeral.

Gradually the jar on the counter filled with the nickels, dimes, quarters and occasional dollar bills of those who had little but who had more than Yogi ever had.

"You'd all do the same for me," one said.

"Yogi would have done the same

thing for any of us if he could have," said another and they all agreed.

There was some talk that Yogi's body could be given to the medical school. Others said the city would bury Yogi, but Big Rock wouldn't hear of it so Yogi was laid to rest in a nice dignified gray metal coffin while the Baptist minister said the prayer, asking the Almighty to look after Yogi now that his friends couldn't.

There were a few flowers in a green vase beside the grave, pink gladiolas from someone's yard. No one knew who had brought them and no one asked. Big Rock had trimmed Yogi's hair one last time and they all agreed that Yogi "looked real good layin' there."

Big Rock left the wreath on the door until it literally fell in shreds one day. He wasn't sure why he had been unable to take it down and fretted continually that they had not been able to learn more about Yogi, had not been able to notify someone who would care that he was gone, someone who had loved a younger, different Yogi.

They managed to get all the bills paid and none of them thought it at all strange that, even in their own lack, Yogi was provided for; and, none of them thought it strange when Big Rock removed the stool from the end of the counter. It had, after all, been Yogi's.

They often mentioned Yogi, always with a smile, always with affection and sometimes wondered aloud if there were people elsewhere in the world who were wondering about Yogi, wondering whatever happened to him.

"Yogi chose to make his way alone," said Big Rock, "either by choice or because he just didn't have anybody he thought cared."

Big Rock thought about that a long time. It just seemed a shame to die and one's folks not even know so one night, after the customers had all gone home, he opened the cash register and under the heavy black metal tray, he placed a piece of paper on which he had neatly printed the names and last known addresses of those who had once shared his life.

He didn't know if they were still at those addresses and he did not intend to find out, but time marched on and Big Rock knew the day would come when his "regulars" would be glad he had left this scrap of blue-lined paper, stained with the grease of his trade. Until then, like Yogi, he chose to walk alone and it was nobody's business why.

"She had learned his name one day while sitting by the fountain in front of the student center, her eyes closed, enjoying the mist spraying gently on her face."

A Stranger Named Kenneth

By the time her daughter left home, grown at last and quite able to take care of herself, life had lost its luster for Lynnette. The position she had worked so hard to attain had become tedious and no longer rewarding. What she had once perceived as prestige she knew now to be a sham. The enviable salary was a trap and the perks were like carrots on the end of a stick with Lynnette, like a donkey, plodding toward them. She had been plodding a long time.

It had been more than thirty years since she left college to marry Bert. Her parents had been furious and they argued, wept, and begged but she would not wait. She could not wait. She would lose Bert who was more important than college algebra, more important than some degree.

Later, after the wedding gown had been fitted and invitations had been ordered, she lost Bert anyway, lost him to someone he described as "someone who really loves me."

"You mean she spread her legs for you," she had said spitefully, for it was in 1963 when girls--at least girls like Lynnette--still "saved themselves" for marriage.

He had told her to keep the engagement ring.

"At least for a while. We don't have to make a final decision now," he had said.

She had thrown the ring at him, marched into her parents' home and shut the door. She eventually married someone else and had been reasonably happy for a time. It was after the divorce that she began chasing carrots, chasing them at first to provide for herself and her daughter but later chasing them for the thrill of the chase and the glory found in the capture.

Lynnette considered all these things until one day she decided to stop being a donkey.

"I've lost my taste for carrots," she stated to the circle of shocked faces when she announced her intention to take an early retirement.

She had enrolled at Wakefield College and the time passed quickly and uneventfully until that day during her final semester when she saw Kenneth and had recognized him at once, recognized him on a level deep within herself though she had never seen him before.

There was great tenderness in his face and he looked as though he knew a wonderful secret, a secret that somehow involved her.

"Hi, Lynnette," he said, but she only saw him speak the words for she could not hear him across the classroom.

"Who was the young man with the red curls?" She later asked students who had been seated around him.

But, even after she pointed to the desk where he had been sitting, no one could remember him and from that day on life became more and more puzzling for Lynnette. She frequently felt as if she were in a dream where nothing seemed quite real and often felt a strange buzzing sensation as if electricity were coursing through her body, though without pain. And through it all, everywhere she went, she saw Kenneth.

She had learned his name one day while sitting by the fountain in front of the student center, her eyes closed, enjoying the mist spraying gently on her face. She looked up and there he was and at that moment someone called out loudly, "Kenneth!"

He had turned as if to wave. Lynnette also turned but saw only the lengthening afternoon shadows across the manicured grounds. Puzzled, she turned back to him but in those brief seconds he had disappeared.

Lynnette had closed her eyes again, lifting her face to the warm sun, listening to the sound of the cascading water and the robins calling to each other in the dogwoods.

She thought she heard a young girl crying, but when she opened her eyes there was still no one in sight.

Every time she saw Kenneth she sensed he was waiting for something, something to do with her. She became apprehensive and tried to avoid him by changing her routine--her normal routes to class, her usual desks in the classrooms--but always he was there and soon he began walking with her from class to class.

She never questioned him but over and over she asked others what they knew about Kenneth. Not one of them could recall having seen him.

"Those red curls? How could you not remember him?"

The answer was always a shrug. No one knew Kenneth.

He said little to her during their walks but the expression on his face was so tender and gentle that often Lynnette felt like crying with no idea why and she decided she must get away for a while and clear her mind of this obsession with Kenneth. She decided to visit her daughter.

It was an unknown voice, though, that answered the phone when she called to let Becky know of her plans. She could hear Timmy, her grandson, crying.

"Is Becky home?" She asked.

There was a soft murmuring as someone tried to comfort the small boy. The hair stood up on Lynnette's arms as she shivered with apprehension.

"Hello? Becky?"

"I'm sorry," the woman whispered. "Becky is still at the hospital. She just called. Her mother died a few minutes ago."

Lynnette dropped the telephone to the floor in horror. Was she losing her mind?

"Lynnette?"

She whirled around to see Kenneth standing there in her own bedroom between her and the windows, the light from them creating an aura around him.

How did he get here?

"What are you doing here?" She whispered. "How did you get in? Who are you? Who are you--really?"

He said nothing, but held out his hand to her and she realized he was not in his customary jeans and T-shirt but wore the most--well, unusual garment.

"Take my hand, Lynnette," he said kindly.

As if in a trance, she reached toward his hand as she knew she must and in that moment remembered the truck on the bridge. It had been the first day of classes and she was late. She had seen the truck coming, careening toward her out of control on the steel bridge. The impact had seemed inescapable; yet, the crash had not occurred. Somehow she had driven on to class that day.

"No," he said softly, gently and tenderly. "No, Lynnette, you didn't."

She stared at him for she had not spoken aloud.

How could he have heard me?

What was happening? Was she having a nervous breakdown? Was that it?

"Take my hand, Lynnette," he said again and the moment her hand touched his it was as if everything was happening at once! She stood there in her own bedroom with its lovely roses everywhere--the coverlet, the ruffled pillows, the pictures.

Yet, the truck raced toward her while to her left was a hospital room and to her right was Wakefield College and beyond that a forest, a forest irresistible in it quietness, its beauty. She could see her daughter, Becky, crying just outside the hospital room as a doctor approached.

"I'm Dr. Gwynneth," Lynnette heard him say. "I'm sorry. We thought she was coming out of it but then her heart stopped. We tried but...."

They were discussing her. That was her body lying on the hospital bed. She recognized it now, but how could that be when she stood there in her own bedroom? It was a dream. It had to be a dream and soon she would wake up and everything would be all right. She turned toward Kenneth who was looking intently at her with just the slightest hint of a smile.

He gestured and Lynnette looked toward the forest and saw a narrow sandy path winding among tall pines and white dogwood, a path lined with huge patches of daisies, bluebonnets, and brown-eyed-susans. It seemed that every flower she had ever seen lay before her as a stream of clear, bubbling water rushed among them.

The sounds were all blending now: The screeching of the truck as the driver braked in terror; the rushing of the water; the sobbing of her daughter; the ticking of her antique bedroom clock. The sounds now all joined together as parts of a whole somehow.

"Who are you?" She asked him again and her mouth never opened.

"All will be made known. Come. It's time," he replied, silently linking his thoughts to hers.

She moved toward the path then and she saw her mother waiting, smiling, welcoming. Lynnette's joy overcame her confusion as she walked down the path toward her mother and others hovered there in the background, others she had known before.

Lynnette, her arms reaching out to her mother, ran then into the beauty, into the quiet peace, into the love which awaited her, into the world of which Earth is only a reflection; and, as she ran, the bedroom with its roses, the hospital room with its sadness, and stranger she had known as Kenneth, all faded away behind her. She never looked back.

"It has been a joy to see Lana's children growing and expanding in the love that Grace showers on them."

Their Special Mother

A year passed before I wept for my sister, Lana. A year of adjustments, feeble attempts at understanding and finally what I thought was acceptance. But I was wrong. I had not reached the point of understanding her death, if indeed anyone ever does nor had I attained any measure of acceptance. Strangely enough, her husband, Tom, showed me the way.

Tom's company transferred him to another office three hundred miles away shortly after Lana's lingering death from cancer. None of us wanted him to move. It seemed unwise to pick up and go so far away with three little girls who had just lost their mother.

"Take the children so far away from all of us? So soon after......?"

"It's an opportunity that may never come again," he said, brushing aside our protests. "The girls will adjust."

"Maybe in a new environment with new friends the girls will adjust even more quickly than they would have where somebody bursts into tears whenever they appear," my husband, Greg, remarked.

I was angered at his words, yet I knew he was right. Tom needed to get his children away from us. Our stifling love only fed their grief.

He brought them back for a visit every now and then on weekends. Each time they seemed a little more distant, more like strangers than the little towheads we had cuddled, scolded, and loved. Tom was polite and friendly but very noncommittal.

"They've come through it pretty well," he would say and that was about the extent of his conversations with us on the subject.

Slowly, but surely, the wounds began to heal. I felt that I had accepted the loss of Lana and the girls at last--until the Saturday afternoon I met the woman who was to become Tom's second wife.

Greg and I were renting a beach cottage for two weeks and had taken the children to the amusement park to ride the Dipsy Doodle. We stood there eating ice cream cones when we saw the vivacious redhead laugh as Tom leaned down to give her nose a light kiss. Fury enveloped me.

"Let's get away from here!"

But Greg took my arm firmly and we made our way through the crowd to where they stood sharing a foot-long hot dog. Tom was surprised to see us but showed no discomfort. I smiled and said all the right things and I held my emotions in check until we left the park and drove back to the cottage.

Throwing myself on the unfamiliar bed, I sobbed. Without a word, Greg handled the baths and got the children into bed but the tears still poured from the depths of my unresolved grief as he came to lie beside me.

The image of Tom and Lana so happy together swam before my eyes. Now it was Tom and Grace. I hated him for his happiness, for replacing quiet, sensitive Lana with someone else, someone so different.

"Maybe if she were more like Lana," I cried, "but it's as though he tried to find someone totally different."

"Marge, you would find it hard to accept anyone Tom might marry," he soothed.

He was right, but somehow I had never even considered the possibility that Tom would remarry. Surely not so quickly! It had only been a little over a year!

"So it's off with the old, on with the new? Just like that?"

"Tom has three little girls who need more than he will ever be able to give them as their father. And he has a right to his own happiness, doesn't he? And you saw how much the girls liked Grace."

Yes, that was another thorn in my

side. How much my nieces seemed to like Grace. Before we left the amusement park they had come running to us, excited about their ride on the Dipsy Doodle. They referred to Grace as "Mom" and, though they seemed glad enough to see us, it was obvious they had given their allegiance to Grace.

"But how could they forget their mother so easily?"

"They haven't forgotten her," Greg said, always the sensible one. "It was bound to be awkward for them at first. After all, when Lana died, Tom lavished everything on those girls. Every nonworking minute the man had was spent with them!

"Then Grace came on the scene and they had to share him with her. That's good, Marge! That's the way it should be. Don't you see? They're a family again and you've got to put your emotions aside."

I knew he was right but I remained bitter. I couldn't forget how much in love with Tom my sister had been. I could still see them that Christmas she brought him home from college to meet the family. Before New Years Day she was wearing an engagement ring and they were married the following spring, three days after graduation.

Lana's husband. Lana's children.

Everything she had loved and treasured all belonged to Grace now and I hated her!

A letter came from Grace shortly after we returned from the beach. Just a note, really: "So glad to have met you. The girls were delighted to see you again. We hope you'll come for the wedding." That sort of thing.

I threw it and the others, which followed into the wastebasket unanswered. Each one reminded me of what Lana had missed and I would lapse into another weeping spell.

It was during one of those spells that Tom appeared at my door. He was in town on business.

"But I had to see you, Marge. I know how you must have felt meeting Grace. You're bound to resent her."

"Yes, I resent her," I said coldly, not wanting to talk to him at all, yet wanting to lash out at him for Lana's sake and so it all poured out of me until there was nothing left to say.

"You're right in everything you say, Marge, but you're also wrong. I loved Lana. I still love the life we had together and I'll never completely get over losing her. But I also love Grace.

"Yes, it's true she's totally different from Lana; but, no one could take Lana's place anyway. Grace has her own place in our lives, the girls and mine. She hasn't tried to usurp Lana's place with them either. She wants them to remember their mother. Her own mom died when she was quite young, so she knows how important it is for them to remember the good times they shared with Lana.

"There have been problems but we've been able to work them out as they arose. I believe this is what Lana would have wanted. Don't hate us anymore."

When he left, I sat down at the kitchen table and wrote to Grace for the first time. We have gotten together, our two families, several times in the two years since that day. It has been a joy to see Lana's children growing and expanding in the love Grace showers on them.

She's into everything, Grace is: Room mother at school, Brownie scout leader, and Sunday school teacher, just everything. Outwardly there are no problems but I know better. All families have problems. My nieces could be more than a handful for Lana and I know they're bound to give Grace a rough time now and then.

But I'm not worried about them and I no longer have any resentment toward Grace. You see, I recently read an essay that my niece had written in school this year on

"My Mother."

My mother has lots of love for everybody and she's lots of fun to do things with. Some people call her our stepmother, but we don't. We call her our "special mother."

Love Is An Action Verb

"It would be so easy," she said. "Just swallow a few pills and simply go to sleep. No need for violence or pain."

I didn't pay much attention to her words. Gave them no thought at all, really. We had been discussing one of the lurid articles that appear with disturbing regularity in our local newspaper about a young woman our age who had committed suicide by driving her station wagon off the side of a bridge after dropping her children at school. A note had been found on her dresser.

"Well, I just don't see how any mother can leave her children like that. How can anyone be so desperate?"

"Maybe she did them a favor," Janice replied.

I was to remember that day with anguish but at the moment I was preoccupied. Besides, the woman in the newspaper had nothing to do with me. I did not know her."

I didn't see Janice for several weeks. We were both tied down with illnesses. Chicken pox, flu and scarlet fever were making the rounds and our kids were exposed to all of them. When we finally got them all back in school, I dropped by to

84

have coffee with Janice and found her weeping and depressed, surrounded by piles of dirty laundry.

"I'm so far behind I'd like to throw it all out and start over," she said, indicating the laundry and stacks of unwashed dishes.

"Oh, it's not that bad," I said, trying to laugh and make light of it all. "Come on. I'll help you get straightened out and then we'll go to the coffee shop. It will do us good to get out. Childhood diseases are much harder on mothers than on children."

When we finished, she threw on an old sweater without bothering to change and we left for the coffee shop. She was quiet. Too quiet. I watched her out of the corner of my eye as I drove. She sat staring out the window, barely commenting as I kept up a steady stream of talk.

I just couldn't seem to stop talking. I had been cooped up with only sick children for companionship and it was good to have another adult to talk with, but why, *why* didn't I let her talk more? She didn't seem to want to and I certainly didn't give her a chance to say much.

"Well, how are you surviving these days?" I asked flippantly.

"Just barely," Janice replied. "I'm not even sure I want to survive any longer."

She spoke seriously, not smiling at

all, but I laughed. I actually laughed! Oh, I was so cheerful, so gay. I was glad to be out again and free of the sickroom. I didn't want to listen to her woes. I didn't want to see her depression. Janice had been down before but she always snapped out of it.

Janice's artistic temperament! Even back in school, she was apt to become extremely depressed. For days on end she would just sit around and sketch--faces, animals, trees--anything and everything. She would sketch constantly, almost feverishly. Then one day she would suddenly snap out of her sullen mood and again be the girl who could do anything, could handle any number of tasks with proficiency.

"Janice, why don't you make this your day? Skip the housework," I suggested as I dropped her off, our coffee break over. "Just take this day for yourself. Gather up your charcoals and sketch pads and just draw today."

"Can't," she said, slamming the door a trifle harder than necessary. "I threw all that junk away."

Why didn't I see it then? Janice had always kept a sketchpad around and would pick up a charcoal as naturally as most people picked up a ball-point pen. Why didn't it bother me that she had thrown it all away? But, no, I was exasperated because she had ruined my first day out after the long siege.

The signs had all been there that morning. How many signs had there been all through the past months? How could I have missed them all?

I had known Janice a long time. She was moody and became depressed easily, but it was understandable. The deterioration of her parents' marriage was bad enough but, in the end, neither parent wanted to keep Janice. There had been no custody fight over the five-year-old child. She was simply taken to a grandmother with whom she lived until she won an art scholarship twelve years later.

She never saw either parent again and she seldom spoke of them. Yes, it was understandable that Janice had experienced many periods of depression during her life and I had grown accustomed to them. They never lasted more than a week or two.

This time, however, she did not snap out of it and I only saw her once more. It was on a Thursday morning and we had gone to a prayer group together. Several of us had been meeting to share problems and solutions and to pray together. The sessions had helped me in coping with things and I felt they would help Janice if she would attend regularly instead of once every two or three weeks.

We were a few minutes late that day and the discussion was already underway.

"Love is the greatest force there is," someone was saying. "To love people is all that is needed. All our problems would vanish if we could just learn to love."

Janice turned and calmly walked out without even sitting down. I followed her to the car where she was waiting, staring straight ahead.

"What's wrong, Janice?" I asked.

When she did not answer, I slipped the gear into drive and eased away from the curb.

"Love!" She blurted. "That's all they were talking about in there! No one really loves anyone else. No one cares what happens to anyone else. Not really!"

She burst into tears and I had never heard anyone sob like that before--deep sobs that shook her whole body, a desolate sobbing.

Somehow I got her home and into the house and she sat at the kitchen table while I brewed tea.

"Is it you and Ron, Janice? Are you having problems? Are the kids getting on your nerves? Is that what's wrong?"

"I don't know what's wrong," she

said, putting her elbows on the table and resting her head on her hands. "I just don't know. I only know that to love is not enough."

Finally I left her. She had stopped crying and said she felt better but I felt uneasy and decided to call Ron as soon as I got home. Maybe he would call her doctor. Get her something for her nerves.

I didn't call Ron, though. I called Janice as soon as I reached my kitchen phone.

"Oh, I'm fine," she said, cheerfully.

Cheerfully? Janice hadn't even smiled the last two times I saw her and now, twenty minutes after I left her, she was cheerful? Why didn't I think that was odd?

"Don't worry! Really! It's going to be all right now."

Relieved, I said goodbye and went back to my never-ending stack of ironing. I had just finished the last piece and was putting the iron away when the phone rang. Janice's two little girls had come home from school and found her on the bed.

"We can't make Mama wake up."

Chills ran over me as I quickly dialed Ron's office but he had already been called. He was on his way home. Snatches of conversations flooded my mind in the minutes before I reached their driveway: *It would be so easy.....Maybe she did them a favor....I don't know if I want to survive.*

So many clues Janice had given to me. Why didn't I see it coming? Why didn't I know?

Ron asked that I sit with him and the children at the funeral. The church was almost filled with people and flowers covered the entire front section.

"She was loved by anyone who knew her," the pastor said. "A loving wife and mother. A good friend to so many."

At the cemetery many came by to speak to Ron.

"She had so many friends who will miss her."

"We've prayed for her so often."

"We loved her."

I wondered if Janice knew she had so many friends. Was she at all aware of the prayers spoken in her behalf? That so many cared?

We grew up together and I was her closest friend. Did she realize I loved her? And if I did love her why couldn't I see all the signs she left on her pathway to self-destruction?

Perhaps they are right when they say it all goes back to her troubled childhood, her rejection and sense of unworthiness. I don't know about all that but I do know Janice was right: To love--to feel love--is not enough. Love is an action verb.

When Miss Sallie Sang

The thing I remember most about sitting in church as a child was listening to Miss Sallie Franklin singing the solos from the soprano section of the choir.

Miss Sallie was my grandmother's closest friend and it was Miss Sallie's singing, which brought them together in a friendship that was to last throughout their whole lives even though Grandmother couldn't even hum a recognizable tune.

The two women met the very day Grandmother and Granddad with their brood of four (going on five) moved into 602 Findly Street.

"Leigh Anne, the very minute your granddad stopped that old Dodge touring car in front of our new home," Grandmother told me, "we heard the most awful sounds coming from across the street you have ever heard and we couldn't imagine what in the world was going on. Well, the expression on your granddad's face would have frightened anyone as he marched himself across the street."

"Some poor soul must be in need of a doctor!" He said.

His face had been exceedingly grim as he marched back across Findly Street.

"The neighbor lady gives voice

lessons in her front room," he growled. "Thank God I'll be at work during the day though I pity you, Gertie, having to listen to that caterwauling!"

They soon discovered that Miss Sallie gave voice lessons every day of the week except Sundays when she sang at Sovereign Grace Baptist Church and on Mondays when she went twenty-five miles into Johnson City for her own voice lesson.

"On Monday nights most all of us on Findly Street sat on our front porches or front steps until the dead of winter drove us inside, because on Monday nights Miss Sallie practiced at home what she had learned that day in Johnson City. How we all loved to hear that woman sing!" Grandmother said

When I came along, Miss Sallie was still singing and she was one of the reasons I spent so much time on Grandmother's front porch. It just seemed to me that Miss Sallie sang all the time. She sang when she swept her front steps, when she fed Big Red, her Irish Setter, even when she weeded her flower beds. I decided she must be about the happiest person I knew.

Our pastor used to say that he never had to worry about attendance at services as long as Miss Sallie stayed in the choir.

"Any time I want to preach an extra

special sermon, I just make sure I do it on a Sunday when Miss Sallie is scheduled to sing a solo and I can be assured of a packed house!"

And it was true because Miss Sallie always sang as if she could see heaven itself and when she sang "My God and I" there was not a dry eye in the entire congregation.

When I was a teenager, though, something happened one Sunday that had never happened before. Miss Sallie's voice broke. We all held our breaths at the dismay on her face and when she closed her eyes, I believe everybody--man, woman, boy and girl, must have prayed right along with her. I know I did.

After a moment or two, Miss Sallie raised her head and began to sing softly in a much lower register than she had ever used and she sang *a capella*. "Amazing Grace" was what she sang and it was the last solo she would ever sing.

It must have been the first outward sign that cancer was developing which would spread throughout her body but none of us knew it then, not even Miss Sallie.

"I'm just getting old," she said, "and it's time for my students to take over the solo work."

Her solos might be ended but Miss Sallie didn't quit singing. The very next

Sunday she showed up in the Children's Department to lead them in singing "Jesus Loves Me" and "Praise Him! Praise Him!" The following week she had organized a children's choir, the first in our church.

"Don't know why it never occurred to me before," she blustered.

Long before I was married and had children old enough for the children's choir, Miss Sallie had demoted herself, as she put it, to the Preschool Department. She had all the four and five year olds so interested in singing and playing musical games, that by the time they entered the children's choir they were old pros.

She often said that the time she spent with the children's choirs were the best times of her whole life.

"Those children," she would say, smiling. "It didn't matter to them if my voice cracked, quivered or croaked like a bull frog. We just went on and made a joyful noise together and praised God as best we could and I don't regret a minute of it."

A joyful noise was about all Miss Sallie could make toward the end but even at the end Miss Sallie sang. As my grandmother sat by her bed and held her hands in those last few hours, Miss Sallie whispered, "Sing with me, Gertie. Let's sing "What a Friend We Have in Jesus."

95

Grandmother, who had never been able to carry a tune in her life and hated for anyone to hear her try, sang with Miss Sallie that day with the doctor and nurses standing around her. She finished the last two lines alone, for Miss Sallie was gone.

People came hundreds of miles to sing in the choir for Miss Sallie's funeral. There were so many music teachers, music students and music directors present that nobody could count them all. They had all gotten their start in Miss Sallie's "front room" or in the children's choirs of Sovereign Grace Baptist Church.

Miss Sallie sang praises to her heavenly Father all her life, and down in our choir room we have a picture of her with her first little children's choir. Underneath the picture is printed her favorite scripture verse: *"I will sing unto the Lord as long as I live: I will sing praise to my God while I have my being."* Psalm 104:33.

*"She stood before the mirror now,
a walking, breathing testimony to the right
dress shops, the right hairdresser and
the right line of cosmetics."*

The Mirror

On the night of her birthday party, Eleanor stood before the mirror and knew she was older than she had ever expected to be. She didn't feel old, didn't feel old at all. In fact, Eleanor felt quite young and happy and she never thought of the pink casket anymore.

It was true that in her younger days she had wanted to die, even had fantasies about dying, fantasies she had never told anyone. As a child she had frequently imagined herself in a soft pink satin-lined casket with her favorite toys beside her as she shut her eyes tightly against the ugliness that was happening, ugliness that hurt so badly, ugliness that could not be spoken.

Eleanor had been sad in those days and her sadness was as much a part of her as the straight brown hair and green eyes. To Eleanor, everything around her had seemed so sad; the shabbiness, the clutter, the dirt, the drabness, the ugliness. Life was ugly and she was ugly and Eleanor would stand before the mirror wondering why she was there, an ugly child in an ugly world, a child who wanted to die.

"Always standing in front of that mirror admiring herself!" Her mother had said. "Miss Prissy Eleanor!"

"Miss Prissy Eleanor! Miss Prissy Eleanor!" Her brothers would sing-song over and over and Eleanor would go into her room and lock the door, shutting herself in and the others out, making her room both a sanctuary and a tomb, longing desperately for something, though she could not have said what it was she craved.

At school Eleanor had walked alone, shunned by the little girls who wore their hair just so with lovely ribbons, who went to piano lessons after school and for a swim at something called "the club." Little girls who did not know the pain and ugliness that came in the darkness of night.

She ate her lunch silently while those around her chatted of things and places she did not know. She read her books at recess, never raising her eyes to see what the others were doing together out on the playground while she sat alone, trying to somehow enter the world of her books, where she could be someone else who was somewhere else-- anyone who was anywhere but *there.*

Yes, Eleanor had dreamed a lot about the pink casket in those days and no one noticed that Eleanor seemed to fade into her sadness as the years went by and she never spoke of the terrible ache. No one knew of her wish to die.

Years later, as an adult, after a

particularly ugly "discussion" with Harold, Eleanor would go into her lovely white and gold bathroom, soak in a hot tub of bubbles and think of the pink satin-lined casket.

Harold had never known, of course. He had thought her quite lucky to be Mrs. Harold Bertnor, thought she should have the good sense to appreciate her status and should be happy with her life and Eleanor had been happy during those first years with Harold. They had met in college where she was studying hard to keep her scholarship and Harold had brought a sense of belonging into her life she had never known.

After their marriage she had put her own family out of her life forever to embrace his, basking in their warmth. Eleanor was a different person then from the little girl who had dreamed of pink caskets. She was more nearly the person she wanted to be, was perhaps meant to be.

Harold's family had cried with her when the two of them moved across country so Harold could enter the law firm of Carter, Morris and Samuels. She knew they loved her, would miss her as much as they would miss their son and she had not wanted to leave that big, happy family but the move had been for the best.

Harold had fit well into the firm and she had been accepted without question by the other wives who had taken her to their hairdresser, their dress shops and their clubs. They had made her one of them and it almost made up for the lack of love between her and Harold. It couldn't, however, make up for the aching bruises which appeared more and more frequently and Eleanor, soaking her aching body in warm bubble baths, began imagining herself once again in the pink casket. Death had once again become a welcome friend who waited close by, waiting for Eleanor to open the door.

The thought of death had stopped after the birth of her first child. Life was full of joy and tenderness and Eleanor didn't want to die after that. She wanted to live and take care of her daughter and the two sons who followed. She wanted to be there to ensure that her daughter wore hair ribbons to school, went to piano lessons in the afternoons. She had to make sure her sons played their favorite sports. She had to be a den mother and she had to take them for swims at the club.

Eleanor lived, and wanted to live, for her children. Now she had lived to be a grandmother celebrating yet another birthday. Never mind which birthday for Eleanor seldom thought of her age in numbers anymore. It just no longer mattered.

101

She stood before the mirror now, a walking breathing testimony to the right dress shops, the right hairdresser and right line of cosmetics. With their help it didn't matter how old she was. Framed by the golden ornate full-length mirror, Eleanor knew she looked good. People said so. She had heard them herself.

"Eleanor looks so pretty," someone had said just tonight, looking only at the expensive gown, the impeccable make-up and hairstyle, not really seeing Eleanor at all.

Letting the sequined dress fall to her feet, Eleanor began to unhook the undergarments, which no one knew were there. Or maybe they did. Could anyone really believe she still had the firm, high breasts implied by her padded long-line?

She giggled at the sight of her breasts hanging there somewhere between where they should have been and her navel, a reminder of the progression of time and the power of gravity. She sighed and squeezed out of the tight girdle.

"I'm not a 'nineties' woman. A girdle is definitely not 'nineties' at all," she said to her mirror, releasing the rolls of extra flesh from their confines.

She lifted the light form of curls and waves from her head and tried to fluff out

102

her own thin, graying strands to no avail; too thin to fluff, too little of it to tease.

Eleanor was glad she had the foresight years ago to have wigs made, matching her own hair color and favorite styles so closely that no one could possibly have known when she quit appearing in public with just her own hair.

The make-up was the next thing in Eleanor's nightly ritual. Off came the blush, the drawn eyebrows, and the salon-purchased eyelashes. Off came the colorful eye shadow to reveal the shadow which life had put there naturally, the shadow acquired from years of worry and strain, shadow that was not pretty.

A far different woman was framed now in her mirror, one her friends would not recognize if she were to walk the streets of her own neighborhood. She spent very little time looking at this person in the mirror. It was an image difficult to accept as herself.

Eleanor reached for her nightgown and yawned as she stepped out of her panties--plain, shapeless, wide-legged things, but comfortable. She turned off the light and took care of the last step of her nightly ritual: Her teeth. (She refused to say "dentures.")

Eleanor could not look at herself in the mirror without her teeth and always removed them under cover of darkness.

Though she never thought of the pink casket now, Eleanor did sometimes consider the possibility of dying in her sleep. She could stand the thought of being seen without make-up and wig, but being seen without one's teeth--well, one could only hope to drop dead somewhere during the day while fully dressed and ready to face the world with teeth firmly in place!

It was odd that after all those sad years of daydreaming about the pink casket she could not even picture it now. It had been so many years since she had even thought about it.

The fantasies had returned when the children were grown and she and Harold had been alone in the house again, but Harold had been dead over twenty years and it was at least that long since she had thought of the pink casket. She had no idea what had made her think of it tonight.

She lay there now listening to the outside sounds, comfortable sounds. A car passed with radio blaring (the neighbor's son coming home from a night out with friends, probably) and somewhere a dog barked, begging to be let in--all comforting sounds to Eleanor, safe in her own canopy bed, enveloped in warmth.

All in all, it wasn't so bad, being this

old. In fact, it was quite comfortable. Yes, she really liked herself now. Eleanor liked herself quite well.

Plain Brown Wrapper

When Julia Thibodeaux announced her retirement and the closing of her beauty shop there was a great stir in the town. It happened on an ordinary Friday in 1953 while Julia shampooed, curled, and combed the women of Rosedale, getting them ready for their respective weekend activities.

"I'm going to close my shop at the end of the month," she had said to each one, just as calm as you please. "I've inherited a small place in the mountains and I'm going to move there and write."

She had, she told them, been writing for several years and wanted to devote more time to it.

They were flabbergasted, of course. None of them had known, had even suspected, that Julia Thibodeaux was a writer as well as a hairdresser.

"What do you write?" They had asked, each and every one.

Julia showed no surprise at their astonishment.

"Oh, short stories, mostly, and--well, other things," she said. "It's just something I enjoy doing. Now that my son is grown and making his own way, I can stop doing hair and just write full-time. I probably wouldn't have the nerve to do it except that

106

they are publishing my book and....."

A book coming out? A book written by Julia Thibodeaux?

"What kind of book?" They had asked her, but Julia wasn't telling. Wait and see," she said. "I think some of you will find it interesting."

The rumors gained momentum (as they were apt to do in a small southern town in 1953) via the telephone party line and along the church pews. Indeed, scarcely anyone heard the sermons being preached in the Baptist, Methodist or Presbyterian churches that Sunday; and, the Episcopalians didn't even bother driving the eighteen miles to Stanfield for their service for fear of missing some vital tidbit of information that might be revealed over the lunch plates at Della Rae's Cafe.

They and the Catholics (those who had made it to early mass that Sunday) were the first to arrive at Della Rae's but their fried chicken, mashed potatoes with gravy and even the fresh peach cobbler sat cold and forgotten as they discussed the question on everyone's mind: *Who did Julia write about in the book?*

Some believed that Julia had written a novel based on the conversations of her clients while she had brushed, combed, and cut their hair. This was almost as disturbing as the rumor that several of Julia's stories had been published in--well, *romance magazines!*

It soon became apparent that there were two types of people in Rosedale: Those who were afraid they wouldn't get a mention in Julia's book and those who were afraid they would. Among the latter were Loretta McLambey, Claire Westlake, and Mavis Kellerbee.

Mavis was the first person Julia had met in Rosedale when she came to town ten years before; but neither Mavis, nor anyone else, had ever been able to learn anything regarding Julia's past. Some said she was a widow, her husband having died early in World War II and they admired her courage in starting her own business and rearing her son alone. No one even whispered that maybe Julia was divorced, for she was simply "too nice to be a divorced woman." No, they all agreed, Julia was a widow all right.

She had appeared one day at the sedate Victorian house on Trent Street to inquire about the "rooms for rent" sign which Mavis had put in her window, a sign everyone in town (including Mavis) pretended wasn't there.

The house had been a showplace and the family prominent during Mavis'

108

girlhood, but she had made a bad marriage and the house was eventually opened to "paying guests," usually young, single schoolteachers. When Julia arrived and made known her plans to open a beauty shop in Rosedale, Mavis decided Julia would open up shop right there on her own premises.

"After all," she exclaimed to her friends at the Rosedale Baptist Church, "we're all tired of having to drive to Stanfield every Friday to have our hair done. It's high time we had our own beauty parlor and you know there's nothing available in this one-horse town for her to set up shop in, so she shall have her shop right there in my front room."

That very same week, Mavis and Jack moved into the rooms to the left of the wide walnut staircase and soon Julia set up shop and housekeeping in the rooms to the right. The front room became a shop with one workstation, two bulky hair dryers and a frightful-looking machine with a dangling apparatus, which was used to give "machine permanents." There were two bedrooms for Julia and her son and they shared the bathroom and kitchen with the Kellerbees.

The arrangement seemed a good one except that Julia had to do the shampooing of her clients in the kitchen since there was no way to install a sink in the front room and the bathroom simply was too small.

"I declare, Mavis Kellerbee, your daddy would turn over in his grave if he saw what you have done to this house," the ladies chastised.

Mavis had to admit that sometimes it bothered her to see the formal parlor where she had practiced her piano lessons now serving as a place of business, but this only bothered her briefly since the excitement of having a beauty shop right there in town and in her own house more than compensated, not to mention Julia's monthly rent check which went straight into Mavis' own little bank account.

"Besides," she said, "Daddy is dead and this is the most exciting thing that has happened in Rosedale for years! With the war in Korea still going on and everybody so down in the mouth all the time--why, we needed this!"

It most assuredly was exciting and one by one, they gravitated to Mavis' front porch to await their turn with Julia. No one was ever in a hurry and Mavis made sure there was always lemonade or iced tea on hand and Julia, more often than not, had a little something in the way of a freshly baked pound cake or molasses cookies. Baking was Julia's hobby.

110

"I don't think I have ever enjoyed having my hair done as much as I have since Julia came." Mavis said, sighing and licking crumbs from her fingers.

They all agreed it was worth the discomfort of having to bend over the kitchen sink for shampoos in order to have their hair done right there in town and made sure to mention at their meetings of the United Daughters of the Confederacy, the mission circles at their respective churches, and the Eastern Star that one of Mavis' paying guests was a dear sweet young widow who was trying to support herself and her child by "doing hair." Those ladies in turn carried the news to the garden club and the Daughters of the American Revolution and Julia's success was assured.

A few of the men, those few who had not gone off to war, asked their wives if Julia was a barber as well as a ladies' hairdresser, but the wives never asked her. Julia was a lovely young woman and there was no need to ask for trouble, though she certainly seemed interested only in her shop, taking care of her son and coming up with new recipes. Baking, she said, calmed her nerves.

She was friendly to all the women and did their hair even when they didn't have the money ("You can pay me when you get it.") and she had all the work she could handle. As for the men, she gave no indication she even noticed them unless one specifically addressed her and then she would speak cordially but kept a respectable distance.

"Julia is a fine woman, a fine, upstanding Christian woman," the women all agreed week after week as they trooped into her shop for curls, manicures, and an occasional facial mask, eager to chat.

Julia never talked much. She just quietly went about the business of making the women of Rosedale as lovely as possible.

"And listening!" Mavis seethed now, talking to Loretta McLambey about Julia's heretofore-unknown sideline. "Listening and writing it all down!"

Loretta said nothing. She couldn't. Every time anyone even mentioned Julia's writing, she tightened up in knots and had to take some of her stomach medicine.

Loretta had gone to Julia's shop from the beginning. Not only did she love the way Julia was able to make her look, but Julia was the only person in Rosedale that Loretta could talk to and feel as if someone really listened and understood. It had been only to Julia that Loretta confided about her sister, Millie, when the knowledge of it became too much to keep within the confines of her own mind.

All Loretta's friends had thought Millie was a young married woman whose husband was out west on some Army post and that she was to join him after her baby was born. Julia was the only one in Rosedale (except Loretta's husband, Fred) who knew that Millie wasn't married at all and that she had been sent to Rosedale to keep the shameful thing secret from her parents' friends and neighbors over in Hopewell County.

"Heaven only knows what we'll all do when the poor pitiful thing is born," Loretta had told Julia, tears streaming down her face, but Julia had given Loretta a little hug, handed her the box of Kleenex and said nothing.

The baby girl was born and it was assumed that Millie was regaining her strength before joining her husband, but then one day there was a wreath on the front door of Loretta's little bungalow. The baby had died.

Loretta, shaking so hard Julia could hardly do her hair the day of the funeral, confided that she just didn't understand why the baby died.

"The little thing was just nursing at Millie's breast with Millie complaining that it was going to ruin her figure. I went to the kitchen to get a glass of milk and a chicken salad sandwich and when I came back the poor thing was dead and there was Millie just staring. Not saying anything, you know, just staring. She said it just stopped nursing and lay still, but I can't help but think--No! I don't dare even think such a thing! It isn't possible! Is it, Julia? I mean, do you think she might have--Oh, no! I'm sure I don't know what makes me even think such a thing! The doctor said some new babies do that, you know. Just stop breathing and nobody knows why. It's just that she never had the slightest motherly feelings for it."

Julia had passed the tissues and tried to assure Loretta that some babies do just stop breathing and no one really knows why, just as the doctor had said. Loretta had tried hard to forget, or at least pretend to herself, that the thing had never happened and she might have been able to do so except for her husband, Fred.

He had resented having "to feed, clothe, and put up with Millie." He knew Loretta's family had always looked down on him so when the undertaker came to make arrangements, Fred made sure the baby would be taken to the family cemetery on

114

the farm just across the county line where Loretta's family lived.

"In the family cemetery," he told Earl, from Barlowe and Son, Mortuary. "Right up front, close to the road."

"You should have heard my mother screaming and yelling at me the day after Earl went up to the house to confirm the exact location before digging," Loretta related to Julia at the time. "She couldn't very well refuse to let Earl bury the poor child so everyone knows all about it now and Mama blames me, of course. They all do. Why, almost none of my folks will even speak to me."

When Fred later realized nothing was being done about a proper stone for the little grave, he took it upon himself to provide one. Loretta thought it awfully kind of Fred and they were standing there the day it was set in place, admiring the sweet little lamb on top of the monument when her mother ran off the front porch and across the corn field carrying a double-barreled shotgun.

"She threatened to shoot if Fred ever set foot on their land again while she was alive," Loretta had told Julia and now with Julia's book coming out......

How could I have told her such private things? Loretta wondered. *What am*

115

I going to do?

The next day, Loretta went to Lanier's Drug Store (where she normally did not shop) and bought two boxes of sleeping tablets. As luck would have it, Claire Westlake had stopped in to get a new pair of nylons for the country club dance the following evening.

"I don't really want to go," she confided to Loretta. "I'm tired of hearing about Julia Thibodeaux's book and I know that's all anybody's going to be talking about!"

Claire was right. There seemed to be more activity in the ladies' lounge of the Rosedale Country Club than there was on the dance floor that evening. One could hardly get through the door, so great was the congestion.

"Well, I can't wait to read the book. I certainly have nothing to hide," someone was saying as Claire pushed her way to the mirror.

They all nodded in agreement, smug in the knowledge that they surely had nothing to worry about and none of them thought anything at all about Claire Westlake suddenly vomiting right there into the dainty lavender sink. After all, somebody was always drinking a little too much and getting just a wee bit sick to their

116

stomachs.

Claire vomited again and again that night after Howard had gone to bed. It was amazing, she thought, what one's nerves could do to the body. She held her throbbing head as she sat on the floor as close to the toilet bowl as possible, pondering the horror of it all. Julia Thibodeaux, a writer! Julia Thibodeaux writing about their lives like that for all the world to see and there was no doubt that Julia would include Claire in the book. She was the only one in town who knew of Claire's affair in years past with Annie Jo Tetherly's husband, Ralph.

Oh, they had broken it off long ago after they found out Claire was pregnant, both of them living in fear of whom the baby might resemble. Those fears were well founded, too. When the baby girl was born and began to grow into a toddler, she looked for all the world like Heather, the daughter of Ralph and Annie Jo. Both girls had the same big brown eyes, dark curls and freckles. Claire's nerves were raw for several years after that birth. For awhile she had thought it might be only her imagination that the two little girls looked so much alike since Claire's own husband seemed to notice nothing unusual. He had bounced the baby girl on his knee just as he had their other three babies.

Yet, on the day she went to enroll her daughter in kindergarten, the teacher saw her child and the Tetherly girl standing together and thought they were sisters! Claire took care after that to display photographs of her family members who had dark hair or freckles and even began to gradually darken her own naturally blond hair. She had held it all inside and her nerves got so bad that her hair had begun to fall out. When Julia mentioned it to her one day while she was doing a perm, Claire just burst into sobs, telling Julia about the whole sorry mess.

For any of this to get out in the public notice now would be disastrous. For the book to come out with this nasty piece of business in it--well, it wouldn't take the whole town long to put two and two together.

It just mustn't be! Claire said silently, staring at herself in the bathroom mirror that night. *I simply won't let it happen!*

Howard was already asleep when she reached, trembling, into his top dresser drawer and gently withdrew his pistol.

I must be the most terrified woman in Rosedale tonight, she thought, staring at the pistol in her trembling hand.

118

One block away sat Mavis, just as terrified as Claire, but Mavis had suffered many things in her lifetime and was not one to panic. She sat calmly, trying to decide the best course of action because it would never do for Julia to have anything in her book about Jack.

Mavis, and her husband Jack, had maintained separate bedrooms for most of their married life and it was to his bedroom/study (which opened right onto the back porch) that Jack had brought his men friends. At first, it was men she knew who came up on the porch declaring they had come to play poker with Jack. Later, it was men she didn't know and didn't want to know.

She had always suspected that poker was not the only game going on behind Jack's door; but, she hadn't been sure until one day she and Julia were sitting on the back porch when two young neighborhood boys came out of Jack's room. She spoke to the boys who mumbled something in return and never looked at her and Julia at all. It was shortly after this that Julia told Mavis she really needed a larger shop and would be moving up the street.

"Besides, with the new health laws, I

can't keep shampooing in your kitchen," she had said. "They'll close me down for sure."

When Julia had moved the last of her belongings out of the front room, she hugged Mavis close and told her to come running if she ever needed help or just needed to talk.

Of course, Jack was dead now, but Julia's book would ruin the family name forever. The shame and disgrace, the pity and whispering of the town was something Mavis just couldn't stand.

Something has to be done. I don't know what--but something!

She went immediately to the telephone and called Julia, asking if they could visit a while.

"I'm already in bed, Mavis, but why don't you come on over tomorrow morning for Sunday pancakes," she said. Mavis agreed and went to bed feeling a little better about the situation. Julia was a reasonable woman and a friend. Surely the matter could be resolved.

A few blocks down Mulberry Street, Loretta decided to take the sleeping pills that sat on her kitchen table. She had no idea how long it would take for the pills to do what they were intended to do so she
120

decided to take them just before retiring. It should be simple enough; she would just go to bed and not wake up again. An accident. It must look as if she had been unable to sleep and simply took a few too many pills.

She intended to finish things properly so she had spent the afternoon cleaning her house from top to bottom. She had laid out her clothes that she would have worn to church the next day and had put her Bible and Sunday School quarterly on the dresser next to her handbag. All was ready.

Satisfied that everything would look normal when they found her, Loretta decided to fix herself a nice little snack and read for a while. She still had a few more chapters of *Gone With the Wind* and she would finish that, put on her best pink nightgown, take her pills and slip under her lovely patchwork quilt for the last time.

She was not nervous. No, she wasn't. It was something that had to be done. She simply could not face the town once this book of Julia's came to the bookstores.

While Loretta denied all traces of nervousness, at that very moment Claire Westlake knew she had gone far beyond any known meaning of the word *nervous* as she hid the pistol in her small handbag and slipped into bed. She had set her little alarm

121

clock to sound well before she and Howard
normally arose on Sundays and had placed it
under her pillow so that only she could hear
it.

Her clothes were hanging on the
bathroom door and she would slip out early
and be waiting when Julia came out for the
morning paper. Of course, after making her
shot, she would then have to turn the
weapon upon herself, but it had to be done
and she was ready to do it. There was no
other way.

It was busy on Trent Street that
Sunday morning. Mavis, eager to get the
messy business over with as quickly as
possible, strode out her front door and down
the street toward Julia's place pondering
what she would say. Maybe she would just
throw herself on the woman's mercy, maybe
plead with her, pointing out what would
happen if all the sordid mess came out about
Jack. Surely it wasn't too late for her to
make revisions on the book.

From a distance, she could see a
figure crouched in the hedge in front of
Julia's house. Mavis wasn't frightened, just
curious. After all, this was Rosedale. There
was nothing to be afraid of in that one-horse
town. There simply was no crime in

Rosedale in 1953.

Just then, the door opened and the figure in the hedge rose and pointed a pistol straight toward Julia as she came down the walk to get her newspaper. Mavis could scarcely believe her eyes. In the split second that followed, she screamed Julia's name and ran toward the two women.

"Claire Westlake, what in heaven's name are you doing with that weapon? Give me that thing!" She said, snatching the pistol.

Claire burst into tears and all three scooted into Julia's living room before the whole neighborhood could be alerted. The two women were trying to calm Claire and fighting a losing battle until Mavis slapped Claire as hard as she could. All three stood dumbfounded, flabbergasted at what was happening but not know what to do or say next.

"Well, will somebody please tell me what is going on here? Claire Westlake, were you trying to shoot me?" Julia asked.

"Yes!" Claire screamed. "Yes! How could you do it, Julia?"

"Do what, Claire? Do what?"

At that moment, someone pounded on the front door as if determined to break it down.

"Well, what next?" Julia fumed,

running to the door.

In burst Loretta, waving her morning paper and pill bottles.

"Julia," she said. "This is cruel, I tell you. Cruel!"

Julia looked blankly at the pill bottles and then at Loretta.

"Why, if I hadn't fallen asleep reading *Gone With the Wind*, I'd be dead right now!" Loretta yelled.

Julia appeared dazed.

"What in the world is going on. Have you all gone crazy?"

"No! You're the one who has gone crazy," Mavis said, "writing a book about all of us like that!"

"You think my book is about you? Is that why people have been acting so strangely? They think I have written about the people in this town?"

Suddenly, she burst out laughing and looked at Loretta.

"Tell them," she said. "I can see I certainly made a mistake by trying to keep it a surprise."

"Oh, it's a cookbook!" Loretta said with scorn. "It's all in the paper today. A damn cookbook and I almost died over it!"

"Let me get this straight," Mavis said. "Loretta, you were going to kill yourself over what you thought Julia was going to say in her book?"

"Yes."

"And you, Claire, you were going to kill Julia over what you thought she was going to say in her book?"

"Well, I thought it would prevent them from publishing the book if she were dead, you know."

They all stared at her.

"I was going to kill myself, too, after I shot her!" She said. "What are you looking at me like that for?"

"Claire, there are no bullets in this pistol," Mavis said.

"Well, Mavis," asked Julia, "why are YOU here this morning?"

Mavis felt her face grow hot.

"Why, just to visit, Julia, and eat pancakes with you, of course," she said, in an effort to portray the picture of innocence in the midst of fools.

Julia had been well-liked, but Rosedale citizens breathed easier when her book, *What's Cooking*, arrived on the shelf of Marshburn's Bookshop; and, when her blue Plymouth drove out of town right behind the Mayflower van, more than a few of them vowed never to tell secrets to another living soul.

"You know, though," said Mavis, a few weeks later as they sipped iced tea on the front porch at Loretta's, "she never did say whether or not the part about her writing for those romance magazines was true."

"Well, no way to tell. Those stories don't give the writer's name," Loretta said.

All heads turned in her direction.

"Well, not that I've ever read that trash, you understand, but my maid did leave her copy here one day. I guess unless you recognized somebody or some situation, you would never really know if Julia wrote it or not."

They all declared as how they weren't about to worry about any such thing as a cheap, romance magazine; but, the workers in the Rosedale post office were certainly amazed at the number of envelopes being sent to certain magazine publishers (none of them with return addresses on them!). Their amazement was nothing compared to the chagrin of certain Rosedale ladies a few weeks later when they found that certain magazines were not delivered, as they had believed, in plain brown wrappers.

Meanwhile, somewhere high in the Blue Ridge Mountains of North Carolina, Julia Thibodeaux sat on her front porch, rolled in a fresh sheet of paper, smiled, and began to type.

126

*"...I want desperately to leave you
something – something of value –
and it has occurred to me that I can!"*

Something of Value

I was in a hurry that day. It was Sunday and I was facing the last week of school with papers yet to grade, exams to give and I was impatient with Mother. I didn't listen.

"I want to go to Pineland Springs, Laura," she said. "Today. We must go today!"

She twisted and re-twisted the blue tissue with shaking hands, ignoring the tears trickling down her cheeks. My mother rarely asked for anything, yet she was demanding and pleading that I take her to some town called Pineland Springs. Why didn't I realize something was wrong?"

"Well, Mama, you'll have to get out of this nursing home first and I have to get through the last week of school before we can go anywhere."

"We can't wait," she whispered. "I need to go now, Laura, before it's too late."

"Now, Mama, that's silly and you know it! You're here just until your hip heals. You're not dying. You're in perfectly good health."

I can't believe I actually scolded her but it was true. Mama was in excellent health and didn't look her age. She had broken her hip by tripping over a pair of roller skates left on the sidewalk by a neighbor's child and she was in the nursing home only because she needed more care than I could give her. She would soon return to the lakeside apartment we shared.

"Why do you want to go to Pineland Springs anyway, Mama? You've never mentioned it before. Where is it?"

"It's --it's just a place I remember, a place I want you to see. We have to go!"

"Then we'll go," I promised. "You talk to Dr. Richardson about this hip of yours and if he says you can travel next weekend, we'll just take to the road and find Pineland Springs."

I pushed her wheel chair slowly to the dining room for lunch with the other patients and their families and there was no chance for further conversation about traveling. I was glad. I just had too much on my mind and I must admit I was miffed that she didn't show any consideration about it. Mama knew how hectic the last week of school was for me every year.

".....and my daughter is a teacher, you know," she was saying to our lunch companions. "She teaches history."

This led to a few polite inquiries but mainly it gave the other patients an opening to talk about their own families. I listened with minimal attention while my mind raced with thought of the work waiting on my desk at home.

Reading and evaluating the genealogies would take a great deal of time because I graded them from several different perspectives.

"....and Laura will be out of school next week......"

Guiltily, I tried to pull my attention back to those at the table who were now preparing to take a walk. Mama and I accompanied them and we all talked of pleasant things, inconsequential things, until it was time for me to leave.

"How are the genealogies this year?" She asked, as I reached for my handbag.

"Wonderful! I'll save copies of the best ones for you to read next week," I promised.

Mama knew how much I loved my genealogy project and she always enjoyed reading some of the papers herself.

"You've always longed to be able to research your own family tree," she said quietly. "I'm sorry about that."

It was one my greatest disappointments but I had long resigned myself to the fact that it was impossible. My mother had told me about growing in St. Bernardette's Home from the time she was a toddler until she was eighteen. She had no memory of family.

St. Bernardette's had burned to the ground in 1942, the year before I was born, she had told me, and since there were no computers in those days, the records had been destroyed as well as the building.

Mama had soon met and married my father shortly after leaving St. Bernardette's, she had explained, but he was killed in World War II before he got her letter telling him of my birth.

"You know, I've never understood why Dad told you nothing about his family," I said. "At least I could have known my paternal grandparents and they could have been a help and comfort to you."

The hurt on her face told me I had said too much. There was much pain involved in this subject and I had never been able to get any answers or understand of that part of Mama's life.

"Anyway," I said, trying to leave on a positive note, "it has enabled me to help my students who are adopted or for other reasons can't trace any of their family. I understand their dilemma.

"Now, Mama, I'll be back on Friday and we'll head for Pineland Springs if Dr. Richardson gives his okay. That's a promise, so you be packed and ready!"

A kiss, a hug, and I left her. She was

at the window as I got into my little blue Escort and I waved. She smiled and watched me turn towards home and the stack of genealogies awaiting me.

It was my favorite part of the class, this genealogy project. It had been my very own idea, the one big innovative idea in my teaching career. I wanted history to be more than just dates and battles to my students so I launched my project.

A few students were immediately interested that first year and the majority of them became interested when I announced that it would take the place of the usual research paper. I was trying to bring history down to the personal level.

I wanted my class to look at history in terms of what was happening during the lives of their own family members which affected their choices in life and, subsequently, have affected the student. My goal was to have them get a better grasp of the implications of history being made today. They would see how their personal choices, our choices as a nation, and choices made worldwide will affect their own great-grandchildren.

Most of the students were fascinated that first year, but there were, as there would be in subsequent years, a few students who resented, feared and dreaded the project.

They were not the only ones. How well I remembered!

"You'd better give some more thought to this project of yours," I was told in the teachers' lounge. "There are rumblings about it. It could cause embarrassment for some of your students."

I had bristled. That project was my baby, my own creation. I didn't want to hear negatives. I knew that some students didn't even know who their fathers were, much less their great-grandfathers but I was convinced that my students would find a source of pride somewhere in their project.

But my principal had misgivings.

"Well, Laura, I just hope we can withstand the onslaught from parents and any other group to take exception to your project. Some people might interpret this as a source of humiliation for those families who are not quite so prosperous, prominent, or even patriarchal. And there's the slavery issue, of course."

"All the more reason for doing it," I had retorted, with more vehemence than necessary. "All my students are intelligent and need to feel pride in who they are and how they became who they are."

I faced my class with confidence.

"To complete your genealogy project," I told the students, "I want you to look ahead. After you see those who have come before you and how their lives have affected yours, consider how your accomplishment, or lack of accomplishment, might affect your children, your grandchildren and theirs. Look at whatever career you think you might pursue, the lifestyle you want for yourself and then project yourself into the future. What might result for your own great-grandchildren from your choices?"

There were problems, of course, but when they arose I worked with the student involved quietly and individually. If there were adoptees in the class, their projects had to be handled from a different perspective, but there were still many positives to be gained.

As I read their findings that first year and watched the enthusiasm evident in their oral presentations, I knew the project was worthwhile.

"They're learning so much more than facts from the encyclopedias and reference books," I reported to the teachers in the lounge. "They're locating family Bibles, old letters and diaries, and they're talking to the oldest family members they can find to get oral histories. They're really learning something and having fun with it."

I enjoyed it as much as the students

did and this year's class gave exceptional oral presentations, so I was full of anticipation for the reading ahead of me as I drove home that day. I gave no more thought to Mother's downhearted mood and her request to go to Pineland Springs.

Had I known what was ahead, I would have taken the next exit and raced back to the nursing home to take my mother wherever she wanted to go. But I didn't know, and the call, which came three days later, was a terrible shock.

"An aneurysm," they told me.

Outwardly, Mama's health had been perfect. Inside, though, had lurked a bubble waiting to burst and take her away. I was now totally alone, alone and filled with guilt. Somehow Mother had known she was about to die. She had tried to tell me and I had been too busy, to preoccupied, to listen.

When the funeral was over and the last friend gone, I sat down to sort through Mama's things. It wasn't until I found it in her purse that I realized I had been searching for something, some final word.

There were her house keys still in the little blue leather key holder I had made for her in girls scouts more than thirty years ago, a small change purse, tissues, and a letter addressed to me.

Dearest Laura,

I don't understand how I know this, but I know you and I will never make that trip to Pineland Springs. No, I don't feel sick. As you said, the only thing wrong is my hip, which, they tell me, is healing quite well. Still, somehow I know I won't be here next weekend.

I'm sorry to leave you alone, darling. I'm so sorry you never married and had children of your own, but you have a rich and rewarding life with your students. You were certainly born to be a teacher!

Laura, I have nothing tangible to leave you except enough life insurance to bury me with, but I want desperately to leave you something--something of value-- and it has occurred to me that I can! I can give you something you have craved all your life--your heritage.

My hands began to shake and I wiped the tears furiously as I read faster and faster.

My darling, I was not brought up in St. Bernardette's as you have believed all these years. I thought it was a necessary lie to tell you and even now I fear your knowing the truth. But, I know your passion for genealogy, your craving for family, so even though I know you will learn certain things,

137

*things I always thought better left unknown,
here it is: Your own family tree, as far as I
know it. It is my gift to you.*

I love you,
Mama

The silence seemed to roar in and
around me as I turned to the last page with
excitement, dismay and even anger, for there
it was, just as she said, my own family tree--
my mother's family.   I stared at the
unfamiliar names, knowing they were a part
of me and I a part of them.   It took me
several minutes to realize my mother had
written her name *Dorothy Olivia Bell* and in
the blank for a husband's name she had
written "None."

Slowly, the realization dawned that if
there had been no husband named George
Allen Mewborne, I wasn't really Laura Rose
Mewborne. I went to my desk to look at the
copy of my birth certificate: Parents were
shown to be Dorothy Bell Mewborne and
George Allen Mewborne. It was obviously
a fabrication and there had been no reason in
the past to question it. Now, rereading the
letter my mother had left, I wept in anger,
despair, and loss.

Mama and I were alone during my
whole life. I had been a "latch-key kid"
before anyone had ever heard the term. She

138

worked every day at a dry cleaning and laundry establishment near our apartment and I would stop by to get the key from her on my way home from school.

Her face was always red and perspiring from the steam pressers surrounding her, but she was always happy to see me, asking about my day at school and giving me pennies for the bubble gum machine. Sometimes she would take her fifteen-minute break to walk the remaining few blocks with me to make sure I settled down to my homework. She was a wonderful mother and we were happy.

Now, I realized I had known absolutely nothing about her and that our entire lives, hers, and mine had been totally focused on me.

Why had she remained silent all those years? Why had I not known the people named on that page? What about Rosetta Bell, my grandmother? What kind of woman ignores the existence of her grandchild? I knew Pineland Springs was where I would find the answers.

Before my clock could sound its alarm the next morning, I was already backing out of my driveway with the map open beside me with the town of Pineland Springs circled in red magic marker. What would I found there? More importantly, *who* would I find there? How does one approach family one has never known?

It occurred to me that perhaps I had been hasty; that I should have made written inquiry first but it was too late. My stomach muscles tightened, my breath came faster and I had to remind myself that what I felt was excitement, not fear, as a few hours later I passed the sign welcoming me to Pineland Springs.

Another sign proclaimed Pineland Springs to be an "All-American City." I wondered what qualifications would designate a town as "All-American" since, driving down Main Street, it seemed as if I had driven onto a set for "The Andy Griffith Show."

That portion of town was so much like the fictional Mayberry that I wouldn't have been surprised to see Andy sitting on one of the porches strumming his guitar or Barney whizzing past me in his squad car!

In front of a barbershop two men actually sat with a checkerboard between them! Nearby was Katherine's Beauty Salon, a small public library no larger than my classroom, and a hardware store where several men leaned, talking among themselves and drinking Coca-colas.

After I passed the last elm on Main Street, it was apparent that I had left the older part of town. More familiar sights greeted me: Fast food restaurants, a shopping strip and self-service gas pumps, even an establishment called the Kit-Kat Klub with garish signs proclaiming "GIRLS! GIRLS! GIRLS!" So, Pineland Springs wasn't *exactly* Mayberry!

At a gas station, old enough to have been there when Mama was a child, I stopped to ask about a place to spend the night.

"Well, there's a Motel 6 up the road about five miles right off the interstate," the woman told me, "or you can stay here in town at the Pineland Springs Inn. By the way, I'm Dottie Meadows and I know you're a stranger because I know everybody in this town."

I admitted to being the stranger and got directions to the Inn.

"Right across the bridge, facing the river," she said. "You can't miss it."

We chatted for a few minutes with Dottie trying to find out who I was and what I was doing there while I tried to find out as much as possible about the town without telling her more than my name.

"Tell you what, Laura," she said. "My husband has gone for a bite to eat and when he comes back, I'm going across the street to the Idle Hour Cafe. When you get checked in over at the Inn, come on back and we'll have dinner together. You don't want to eat alone, do you?"

I certainly didn't want to eat alone with my emotions in such turmoil. Besides, I liked this woman. Years of meeting parents had given me a sixth sense about people so I agreed to meet her later.

Locating the Pineland Springs Inn was easy. Rounding a curve beyond the bridge, I turned at the faded sign and saw immediately that while the inn would certainly provide a place to sleep, it was most definitely not the sort of place I had always envisioned with the word *inn* was spoken. It was on the river, which was about the best I could say since its paint was peeling, the decor non-existent and the desk clerk less than hospitable.

I guess my emotions over the past few days had taken their toll not to mention the fatigue from driving several hours without rest, because I actually burst into tears when I saw the room. The white painted iron bed, the desk and chair were all of dubious strength and had probably come from a yard sale. I barely heard the clerk telling me the bathroom was "down the hall and to the right."

I didn't feel much better after trotting "down the hall and to the right" for a shower but I donned a clean skirt and blouse anyway and drove to the Idle Hour which was already filled with patrons, all staring at me as I crossed the room to where Dottie sat, waving a menu.

"You'll want to look at this," she said, "but I can tell you that you can't go wrong with the stuffed pork chops."

I went along with her suggestion and then turned my attention to the restaurant itself. As with the inn, the decor was absent. The tall dark wooden booths must have been there at least since 1950 though the tables, which sat near the counter, were newer, perhaps 1960! (Red Formica tabletops!) I noticed the certificate given by the State Board of Health showed *Grade C*.

"So are the Idle Hour and the Pineland Springs Inn owned by the same person?"

"Oh, don't worry!" Dottie said, laughing. "Bill always gets a "C" because he never gets around to replacing the broken tiles on the floor or putting his garbage cans on racks but his cooking is superb!"

She was right. I was enjoying food, as I hadn't for several days.

"So why are you in Pineland Springs?" She asked, point blank. "And don't say just passing through because no one just passes through Pineland Springs.

You had to get off the interstate and drive fifteen miles to get here. So why?"

I didn't know what to say since I wasn't sure myself, but I began pouring out everything to her, the way we do sometimes with strangers. I told her all about Mama in the nursing home, our life together, that I had always thought we were alone in the world until now.

"But now that I'm here, Dottie, I don't know how to begin. I'm frightened about this whole thing but I have no idea what it is that frightens me."

"Well, you poor thing! All that you've been through and I had to send you to the Pineland Springs Inn!"

It was good to laugh with someone again and feel some of the tension draining from me.

"So, tell me, Laura. I know you came because it's your mother's hometown but who *was* your mother?"

"Her name was Dorothy Olivia Bell."

I showed her the letter I had found in Mama's purse.

"*You* are Dorothy Bell's daughter?" She asked, staring at the letter in disbelief. "Why, I was named after your mother. She was my mom's childhood friend! Come on! I'll show you where she lived, where your

144

grandmother still lives. You won't want to go there right now, of course, but at least you'll know where to go tomorrow bright and early. You'll need to go when you're fresh, believe me. Rosetta Bell is--well, you'll see for yourself!"

Dottie paid our check and I drove while she gave a running commentary on everything and everyone we passed until we came to a section where all the houses boasted sprawling, wraparound porches and were set well off the street with their backs against the river.

"That's it," she said, pointing. "That's the Bell place. Drive slower. Miss Rosetta is probably walking by the river. She's always walking there."

The once white paint was peeling and the lawn needed attention but it was still a lovely home. With the river behind it and two huge oaks in front, the house presented quite a different picture from the small places Mama and I had always lived. How awful that must have been for her, after living in a home such as this.

I tried to picture her in the porch swing as a young girl and walking by the river with her friends. Was she a tomboy who climbed the branches of the oak trees?

"There she is!" Dottie cried, bringing me out of my reverie. "That's Rosetta Bell over there, walking by the river."

Could that woman really be my grandmother? I couldn't imagine a less grandmotherly type. Rosetta was tall, stylishly thin and stylishly dressed. And severe. Even using a walker for support, she had a stiff haughty carriage and her hair was pinned up just so.

"I'll bet her clothes wouldn't dare wrinkle," I said to Dottie and, in spite of myself, I shivered, feeling no pleasure at the prospect of meeting this woman.

As a child I would have loved coming here, having a swing among the branches of an oak or maple, having my grandmother rock me in one of the white wicker rockers, and floating a boat on the river.

I had a strong suspicion, however, that Rosetta Bell would never have allowed a swing in one of her trees and that she wasn't the rocking type, regardless how many rockers might be on her front porch. I don't think she would have encouraged summer visits from a little girl and I tensed even now to think how she would feel about a grown-up granddaughter.

I drove into the driveway at 142 Riverview Drive shortly after nine the next morning but instead of my grandmother, a uniformed maid met me at the front door informing me that Mrs. Bell was "not seeing callers this morning." Did I "wish to leave a message?"

Reminding myself that my grandmother had apparently ignored the fact of my existence for my entire "forty-something" years, I decided not to allow myself to be intimidated or ignored any longer.

"No, I do not wish to leave a message. Please tell Mrs. Bell that her granddaughter, Laura Rose Mewborne, is here to see her."

The look of amazement on the woman's face was nothing compared to the anger on the face of Rosetta Bell when she came into the foyer where I had been left standing.

"Who are you?" She demanded. "How dare you come into my home and say such a thing! I have no granddaughter."

"Did you not have a daughter name Dorothy Olivia Bell? Well, then, you have a granddaughter and she is standing in front of you!"

We stared at each other until finally she broke eye contact.

"Come into my sitting room." It was like a royal command.

In spite of my anxiety, I found the "sitting room" enchanting. Though spacious, the room was made cozy with a floral camelback sofa with ruffled skirt, big easy chairs covered in solid green slipcovers and flowers. Real flowers. No silk arrangements in that house!

Floor to ceiling bay windows flanked the French doors leading to the screened porch overlooking the river. Built-in bookcases, again floor to ceiling, and a large fireplace framed by intricately carved mahogany made up one complete wall and as I looked around this wonderful room, I felt a sudden ache akin to homesickness, a longing for something I never had.

"So. You've come here blatantly, uninvited and unannounced. Why?" She asked. "And where is your mother, if indeed Dorothy is your mother? Did she not have the courage to come here and face me? Where have the two of you been all these years?"

In the split second that followed, I decided to be as bold, blunt, and unfeeling as she was.

"My mother is dead," I said, clearly and distinctly. "She died a week ago and though I am your granddaughter, I am an adult so don't speak to me as you would to an errant child."

For a fleeting moment I saw something cross her face. Shock? Dismay? Pain? I wasn't sure what it was, so quickly did it pass. However, she did soften toward me and apologized for her brusqueness.

The coffee was brought in at that moment so I was given a few minutes to gather myself and think carefully what I was going to say. When the maid, Anna, left the room, I began to tell this woman about myself and about her own daughter. I told of the struggles we had when I was small and how Mama had provided me with so much love and happiness and how the situation had reversed itself when I graduated from college and started teaching.

"Why did she never contact me?" She blurted. Why did she never tell me where she was, that she had a daughter? Why didn't you contact me when you got older?"

I showed her the letter, which she read, the pages trembling in her long, bony hands.

"As you can see, I knew nothing of Mama's past or family until a few days ago."

"It's Dorothy's handwriting. I'd know it anywhere," she said.

I told her of my last visit with Mama and of her asking to come to Pineland

149

Springs. To my shame, I burst into tears.

She made no effort to comfort me.

"I'll show you Dorothy's room," she said, rising and moving toward the stairs in the vast hallway.

She rode the chair lift as I walked beside her up the mahogany staircase.

"It's exactly as she left it," she said, motioning me toward the room.

The antique furniture was dark, large, and heavy but everything else in the room showed that a young girl had lived there. School pennants on the wall, frilly make-up table, with a silver brush and hand mirror. Even her magazines were still on the bedside table. They would be collectors' items by now.

"You expected her to come back," I said, turning to look at the woman who stood in the doorway. She would not come further into the room.

"We've even kept the same curtains all these years. We take them down to wash and iron every spring and fall. Everything is the same."

I walked over to the pictures on the night table. Pictures of my mother as a young teenage girl with her friends and one of a very handsome boy stood on the table.

"Was this my father?"

"No. I don't know who your father

was and I doubt your mother knew."

I turned to retort but she was already on the stairs.

"Come along, " she said over her shoulder. "We'll walk by the river."

When we were as far as we could get from the house without actually being in the river, she spoke again.

"Look, my dear, you have come here for good reasons, I think. You have come to learn who you are and who your family is but you have to understand that there was good cause for your mother to keep her past from you. It has been so long now, over fifty years and some things are better left alone."

She almost broke then. I could see it in her face, but more than eighty years of rigid living, rigid thinking and complete control of her emotions helped her to remain composed as the words began to flow from her as if a dam had burst. She spoke of my mother's birth and childhood. Cute things. Sweet memories.

"Dorothy was such a sweet girl growing up but something happened when she was twelve. I didn't know what was wrong. She would hardly speak to either of us, her father or me, and she seemed to stay away from home as much as possible, usually with her friend, Blanche.

"When she was home, she stayed in her room almost all the time coming down only grudgingly for meals. I took her to the family doctor who advised she was just entering the difficult years young girls face and that she would grow out of it.

"She didn't, though. If anything, she became more withdrawn, just never looked happy. I didn't know what to do. She wouldn't tell me anything, wouldn't talk to me at all if she could avoid it.

"Then, after she entered Pineland Springs High, it was as if she just went wild. I was forever being called by the principal. One day he told me Dorothy was slipping off campus to meet boys. I asked what boys. He said some from town here but a lot of them he didn't know."

I was stunned. The girl she described sounded nothing like my mother. I couldn't believe it.

"I can see you don't believe me," she said, shaking her head. I didn't either at first and even gave Mr. Ledfelter, the principal, a tongue-lashing at saying such things about my Dorothy."

I nodded for there was no doubt in my mind that Rosetta Bell could give a tongue-lashing *extraordinaire*!

"I talked to her, or tried to talk to her. She sassed me every time I tried. When

152

her father found out, he took a belt to her. Yes, I can see you're horrified, but that's the way he was, you see. Said there was no way he was going to tolerate a trollop for a daughter and he would see to it she behaved herself. The beatings did no good. No good at all.

"Her grades plummeted, but she didn't care. When they caught her on the school bus stark naked with one of the football players, I just broke down in the school office and told the principal I didn't know what to do anymore and begged him not to tell her father."

The rest of the story made me sick to my stomach, literally. The principal had decided that a dose of public humiliation might solve the problem since the private beatings had done no good at all, so he called a special assembly of the entire student body and faculty. He then made the young Dorothy stand on stage and "apologize" for her "shameful behavior." She had to say she was a tramp and beg forgiveness of her fellow students for disgracing their school.

My horror must have been evident for she reminded me it had been 1942 and "morals were stricter than in the schools today."

"Mrs. Bell--Rosetta--well, I don't

even know what to call you, but I can tell you this. I have been a teacher for over twenty-five years and I have never seen any student who deserved public humiliation like that. Not one. That principal was an absolute sadist. How could you allow him to do such a thing?"

Whether my tears were from anger or from the pain I felt for my mother's experience, I did not know. I did, however, recognize a growing feeling within me, a suspicion of something, though I knew not what. At that moment, I only knew I wanted to get away from this woman who had failed her daughter, who had caused untold pain by allowing beatings and then public humiliation. No wonder my mother never returned to this place and kept all this from me.

I turned and left her without a word and drove straight to the inn where I dropped into bed and straight into a sound sleep, the sleep of the emotionally exhausted.

Dottie called shortly before five o'clock pulling me from the depths of my dreaming.

"So, how did it go today?"

I mumbled something. I don't remember what.

"Look," she said. "We all know

Rosetta Bell, so I know it was a rough day. I want you to come to my house for dinner tonight. My mother is coming, too."

I said I didn't feel up to going out but she threatened to come get me if I didn't show up so I jotted down the directions, grabbed my terry robe and headed back down to the hall to the shower.

The soothing warm spray could not calm the turmoil, still vague and nameless, which I had carried with me into sleep and still remained with me. My pain for what my mother had endured was unbearable and I was glad she did not live to come back. I could not imagine any reason she would ever want to come back, until I met Dottie's mother, Blanche.

"Oh, Laura, I just loved your mother!" She exclaimed the minute I walked into Dottie's den with its bright plaids and comfortably worn furniture. "Well, of course, you must know I did since I even named my daughter after her! Now, come on and let's chat while Dottie gets dinner on the table."

Blanche was a chatterbox and I was regaled with stories of her and Mama as little girls and then as teenagers but I was confused. The person she described was more like the mother I knew, a quiet, kind-hearted person who loved to read, who liked

155

to do needlework but who also loved to laugh and play. I just couldn't reconcile the description given by Rosetta Bell with the mother I knew, the person Blanche was describing, and I said so.

I could see Blanche was uncomfortable but I pushed her to speak the truth.

"Your mother was a wonderful friend, Laura, but there were things that bothered her, things she never talked about because--well, you have to realize that some things were not discussed in our day as they are now."

"Well, Rosetta says it all started when Mama was about twelve, that she became very withdrawn about that time."

Blanche remembered the situation well.

"Yes, she was at our house a lot," she said. "She spent the night frequently. We had a lot of slumber parties with lots of girls eating, dancing, and gossiping. Precious little slumber took place!"

"But, Rosetta said that Mama was wild in high school. That her father called her a trollop, a tramp, and actually beat her with a belt. Did you know about that?"

Blanche turned to me, took me by the shoulders and said, "Laura, Your mother was a wonderful girl."

Her look made me hesitant to even want to hear but as I pulled away from her, something in my brain clicked and in that instant I knew what she was reluctant to say. Our school system has taken great pains to give teachers training on how to recognize children who have been molested and over the years I had seen students in my classroom who became withdrawn and excessively modest seemingly overnight and still others became promiscuous--behavior totally out of character for each of them.

As Blanche spoke the words, though, I could not be objective or calm and she held me close as I clung to her.

"You shouldn't have heard this so soon after losing her," she said. "I shouldn't have told you."

She said Mama confided her situation when Blanche once innocently remarked how much she liked Mama's father.

"Because he was so nice and was always hugging us and telling us how pretty we looked. Dorothy started crying when I said that. Then she revealed to me what happened at night in their home. She had asked for a lock on her bedroom door, but Rosetta chided her for being a baby, afraid of the dark,

"But you can't blame Rosetta, Laura.

157

I'm sure she had no idea what was going on."

"And if she had known? What would she have done?" I asked. "The same thing she did when he beat her daughter with the belt? Nothing? The same thing she did when they made her daughter get up on that stage in total humiliation? Nothing? Couldn't anyone see what was happening? Couldn't anyone help her? A minister? A teacher? Somebody?"

"Well, Laura, you have to understand. Such things were not discussed openly at that time. I don't think Dorothy had faith that anyone would believe her. Not the minister, not her mother, not a teacher, not any adult."

I couldn't take any more knowledge of the past or even any more kindness. I had to get out of there. Why hadn't I just left well enough alone and simply kept the wonderful memories Mama and I shared? Instead, I had opened Pandora's box.

"Well, I'm going to tell her. I want her to know how my mother suffered, what she endured. I want her to know how she failed her daughter," I told Blanche as I stood to leave.

"Don't do it, Laura," she urged. "She's an old woman. It can't help your mother now and it could kill Rosetta."

158

At that moment I didn't care.

I awoke my second morning in Pineland Springs to a gray sky and rain pelting the windows. The little radio I had brought with me gave news of a nor'easter headed our way and that this rain and wind was but a foretaste of what was to come. It matched my spirit perfectly.

Lying there, dreading to get out of bed, I pondered my next action. Some of my anger had abated but my sadness for Mama's life was overpowering. I tried to piece together what had happened but could only surmise that after school was out, my mother had gone to the city, found work, met my father and just never went back or contacted anyone. Whether or not she was pregnant before she left Pineland Springs or became pregnant later was irrelevant at the moment. I was not yet ready to consider that there might never have been a George Allen Mewborne at all.

I assumed she tried to put it all behind her and when I was born she just wanted to protect me not only from her father, but also from the knowledge that she had been a different person from the mother I was to know.

So! I had found my family at last.

Now what? I still wanted to tell Rosetta Bell the truth. I wanted to inflict pain on her. I did not care that she was old and feeble now.

She was the mother. She should have known what was happening and she certainly should not have stood by while her daughter was being beaten. And she should never, never have allowed the principal to make a public spectacle of her child.

Could people have been so blind, so ignorant, in 1942 that they could not see a girl with serious problems? Couldn't anyone have reached through that early silent shell or the later wild facade?

The harsh ringing of the telephone brought me back to the present. It was Rosetta's maid calling at eight-thirty in the morning.

"Mrs. Bell wishes you to have breakfast with her."

Making my way up the brick walkway to her front door, I could hardly believe that it had scarcely been twenty-four hours since I had rung that bell the first time. Twenty-four hours, a lifetime ago.

She opened the door herself this time and this time she looked like the old woman she was. Age was upon her face as I had not seen it the first time. Age--and something else--something no cosmetic could hide. She knew the truth.

160

As we sat down to the frilly, perfectly set breakfast table on the back porch, we could see a lone sailboat taking advantage of the wind from the incoming storm, its crew ignoring the pelting rain.

"Dorothy loved to sail, you know," she said, buttering her toast, hands shaking.

"No, I didn't know," I replied with as much coldness as she had shown the day before. "We had no opportunity for sailing in our lives."

She went on as if I had not spoken. I'm not even sure she heard me.

"Yes, she and her father used to sail every weekend that there was the slightest bit of breeze out on that river. Then, abruptly, around her twelfth birthday she just lost all interest. He tried to get her to go out, but she refused and finally he quit asking her and sold the boat."

She did not raise her head as she kept buttering the already buttered toast and I began to feel queasy, the hairs on my arms were full of electricity and I had difficulty swallowing my coffee. She knew. There was no doubt about it. She knew and she had done nothing about it.

"I loved my daughter, my sweet little Dorothy," she whispered.

I stared, hardly believing she could say such a thing. I hated her. I could not be tolerant for this old woman. I ached for the little girl who knew no one would believe her, ached for the lively teenager whose defensive rebellion cut her off forever from everyone she knew.

I hated all those who had hurt the child who had become my wonderful mother, but most of all I hated this woman, the one person who had charge of that little girl, whose responsibility it had been to care for her and to protect her. The woman, who in the end, left her to the sadistic and ignorant "discipline" of a school official.

"Did she graduate that year?" I asked, silently daring her to raise her eyes and look at me.

"What? What did you say?"

"I asked you if Mama graduated that year."

"On, no," she whispered. "She never even came home that day. After she had to go on the stage and......she just never came home at all."

I could not let it go.

"You know, of course, she was molested by your husband, her own father."

Still she did not answer, but sat with head bowed, looking only at her toast, now cold and soggy with the butter and fancy jam.

"Why? Why did you let it happen?

Why didn't you do something? How long did you know?"

She flinched at each question as if I had struck her, but she did not answer.

"You didn't even try to find her, did you?" I asked, standing to leave, disgusted.

She looked at me then and I saw with perverse pleasure that I had broken through that haughty facade that created awe in all of Pineland Springs. I, alone, saw the pathetic lonely woman who had lived a lie for most of her life, hoping and praying that no one had guessed the truth.

"You will come back, won't you?" She asked, beaten at last and grasping for my hand. "I know you're suffering and the things you have learned here have made your grief doubly hard to bear, but after you have mourned her, you will remember that you made her life happy. Even if you hate me, come back."

Yes, Mama had been happy. She spent more of her life being happy than she did in Pineland Springs being sad and I still couldn't understand why she wanted to come back to this awful place.

I drove back to the inn, paid my bill, packed my things in the car and drove over to say goodbye to Dottie. As I drove slowly down Main Street on my way out of town, the chimes in the white brick courthouse were striking eleven o'clock.   It was a comforting sound, an innocent sound, and the town looked so lovely, at least this part of it. Was that why Mama wanted to come back? To see her childhood home again? Was it Blanche she wanted to see? Could she possibly have wanted to see Rosetta? Had she been trying to ensure that I was not alone?

I knew the answer to those questions lay at the house on the river. I turned and drove back to that house.

Rosetta was again walking by the shore, weeping while the wind from the approaching nor'easter tore at her hair and clothes and the rain mingled with her tears. Was that why she walked by the river so much? To weep where no one could see? How many years had she wept alone uncomforted?

I had to go to her. I held her close to me that morning as we both looked out over the river, unable at that moment to look at each other.

"I think Mama wanted to let you know she had forgiven you," I said gently. "I believe this because never in her whole life did she show the slightest bitterness or sadness. She truly had inner peace."

Perhaps as death approached and gave my mother warning somehow, she realized she needed to release Rosetta from her own pain and guilt--a mother who had failed her child. When I looked into my grandmother's face I knew I had done it for her. I had completed the thing my mother wanted to come back to do.

Driving home that day I considered just how painful my genealogy project might have been for some of my students through the years. What pain had they encountered as they went exploring through family trees? Without exception, they had exhibited pride as they presented their finished work and as they talked about their findings. None of them ever seem distressed when the project was over.

Why then, after this initial effort at delving into my own family tree, did I feel such pain, such sadness, over what had been and what might have been? How had my students reconciled their hurts, the unpleasant things that can be encountered when one begins looking into the past?

When I walked back into my apartment and looked around at the little touches left by Mama which had made it "home," I thought I knew--or hoped I knew!--what my students had discovered: The power of the human spirit to endure, overcome, and blossom.

I would grieve for my mother for a

long time but I knew she had been happy
and fulfilled and had triumphed over the evil
in her life. I knew, too, that I would
overcome my grief and my rage. I would
return to Pineland Springs one day. I had
found my family and I had a genealogy to
write.

Author's Notes

Note one: "Three Letters from Teddy" was first published in the March 1976 issue of *Home Life*. It has been almost continuously in print somewhere since that time in many magazines and anthologies as well as in the course packs in the schools of education at several universities. In her 1994 Annual Report of the Children's Defense Fund Marian Wright Edelman used it and Senator Dan Burton requested reprint rights in order to have the piece distributed to educators in his district. I have received much correspondence about this story and I believe it is because so many of us have experienced being a "Teddy" or a "Miss Thompson" at some point in our lives. Many of us have experienced both.

Note two: "The Christmas Nandina" first appeared in the anthology, *Stories For a Woman's Heart*, Multnomah Publishers, 1999.

Note three: "Their Special Mother" was first published in *Home Life*, June 1977.

Note four: "Love is an Action Verb" was first published in *Home Life*, July 1976.

Note five: "When Miss Sallie Sang" was
originally published in *The Gospel Choir*,
Jan/Feb/March 1980.

Author's Biography

Elizabeth Silance Ballard-Ungar's short stories and articles have appeared in many magazines since 1974 including *Our State, The Australian Women's Weekly, Home Life, Mature Living, Mature Years, The Organist, The Church Musician, The Organ Portfolio, The Music Leader, The Gospel Choir, The Lutheran Woman, The Lutheran Scope, The Mennonite, Quaker Life* and many others. Her articles have also appeared in *The News and Observer* (Raleigh, NC) and the *Jacksonville Daily News* (NC) and her devotionals have appeared on *Open Windows and The Church Musician.*

Several anthologies have included her work including *A Second Helping of Chicken Soup for the Soul* (credit was omitted in the 1st printing but corrected in the 2nd printing), *Stories for a Woman's Heart, More Stories for a Woman's Heart, Stories for a Teacher's Heart, Stories for a Teen's Heart, School Bells and Ink Wells, Kisses of Sunshine,* and others. Her work has also been included in other works such as *Divergent Views on the Control of Schools: An Iowa Dialogue, Discipline for Life* and others.

Her short story, "Three Letters from

Teddy," first appeared in 1974 and has been almost continuously in print every year since that time in various publications. Marian Wright Edelman selected it to appear in her 1994 Annual Report of the National Children's Defense Fund. Congressman Dan Burton, Indiana, requested permission to have the story reprinted and distributed to every educator in his district. It has also been selected for the course packs of the schools of education in several universities including the University of South Florida, UNC-Greensboro, University of Northern Iowa and others.

She has also co-authored a book, *Whoopin' and Hollerin,'* a collection of humorous, nostalgic pieces by Elizabeth and her sister, Hilda Silance Corey, and their mother, Estel Stanley Silance about growing up in the south and spans a time from the early 1900s through the Sixties.

Elizabeth is a retired social worker, a church organist, a pianist, and is the mother of two and grandmother of three. She has traveled extensively in the U.S. and abroad and enjoys reading,, writing, needlework and line dancing. She is active in her church and the Order of the Eastern Star.

Printed in the United States
72521LV00001B/103-198